Black Helicopters

BOOKS BY CAITLÍN R. KIERNAN

Agents of Dreamland (available from Tor)
Cherry Bomb (as Kathleen Tierney)
Red Delicious (as Kathleen Tierney)
Blood Oranges (as Kathleen Tierney)
The Drowning Girl: A Memoir
The Red Tree
Beowulf (novelization)
Daughter of Hounds
Murder of Angels
Low Red Moon
The Five of Cups
Threshold
Silk

BLACK
HELICOPTERS

CAITLÍN R. KIERNAN

A TOM DOHERTY ASSOCIATES BOOK

NEW YORK

BLACK HELICOPTERS: AUTHOR'S DEFINITIVE EDITION

Original edition copyright © 2015 by Caitlín R. Kiernan in *Beneath an Oil-Dark Sea* (Subterranean Press)
Expanded, revised edition copyright © 2018 by Caitlín R. Kiernan

Cover photograph of Sedgwick, Maine © Don Seymour/Getty Images
Cover design by Christine Foltzer

Edited by Jonathan Strahan

A Tor.com Book
Published by Tom Doherty Associates
175 Fifth Avenue
New York, NY 10010

www.tor.com

Tor® is a registered trademark of Macmillan Publishing Group, LLC.

ISBN 978-1-250-19112-0 (ebook)
ISBN 978-1-250-19113-7 (trade paperback)

First Edition: May 2018

For Sixty-Six

One measures a circle, beginning anywhere.

—**Charles Fort**

Sometimes the questions are complicated
and the answers are simple.

—**Dr. Seuss**

Black Helicopters

1.

Radio Friendly Unit Shifter

Here's the scene: Ptolema sits alone in the booth at Bewley's Oriental, sipping bitter black coffee. The October morning sun makes hard candy of Harry Clarke's stained-glass windows, and she checks her watch, and she stares into her coffee cup, and she looks at the stained glass, in that order, over and over again. The two agents are late, and late could mean anything. Or it could mean nothing at all. She's surrounded by the clamor of Trinity students and faculty, locals, tourists, latter-day bohemians. Ptolema hasn't been in Dublin in almost twenty years now, and it made her angry and sick to her stomach to see the Starbucks that's opened almost directly across the street from Bewley's. This thoroughfare is no longer the Dublin of James Joyce and Oscar Wilde, not the Dublin of Mícheál Ó Coileáin and the Easter Rising. Grafton Street, she thinks, might as well be a Disney

World reconstruction of the city. It was not so far along, this cancer, the last time she was here. But, again, that was almost twenty years ago. This is Dublin attempting to remake and sanitize itself for the World At Large, for the travelers who want history as exhibit, local color free of anything that would make them uneasy. Plastic Paddy souvenirs. Leprechaun and shamrock tchotchkes. But, Starbucks or no Starbucks, the McDonald's at the intersection with Wicklow Street or no, Burger fucking King or no, a block or two in almost any direction, and that, that is still Ewan MacColl's "Dirty Old Town," sure as Salford ever was.

> *Heard a siren from the dock.*
> *Saw a train set the night on fire.*
> *Smelled the spring on the smoky wind.*
> *Dirty old town, dirty old town.*

And even here on Sráid Grafton, there are still the buskers, the street preachers, the children sent out by their parents to beg for spare change. Stand on Ha'penny Bridge, and the Liffey still brings to her mind Murdoch and how "No man who has faced the Liffey can be appalled by the dirt of another river." The tourist-friendly cancer is kept hemmed in by the disagreeable, living city that will never have its face scrubbed up presentable for company. So, good for you, Dirty Old Town.

I want to give a picture of Dublin so complete that if the city suddenly disappeared from the earth it could be reconstructed out of my book.

Ptolema checks her watch again: 10:38 a.m., which puts the X agents almost a half hour tardy. She's already called her handler in London once, and if she calls again Ptolema knows she'll be pulled. Because it could be a setup. Because it might be. She turns off her phone, just in case Barbican Estates decides to ring her. There's too much riding on this meeting, and she's not about to see three months' work swirl down the shitter because someone can't tell time. Or can't be bothered. This is, of course, to be expected from the X motherfuckers, and she knew that going in. She leans back in the booth, wanting a cigarette, and the air smells like frying eggs and dry little disks of black and white pudding.

Watch face. Coffee. Stained glass.

She bought the watch from a Munich pawnshop in 1963. The steaming coffee reminds her of the mist rising from that bay in Maine that has disgorged Hell's own derelicts. The windows hint at an unfamiliar world.

Ptolema notices four students at a nearby table staring. Laughing amongst themselves. Sniggering boy-men. Muttering German. One jabs a thumb her way. To those pasty, pale bastards, she must cut a strange sight, sure:

bald head smooth enough it glistens in the sun through the windows, her brown skin, the ugly scar over her left ear, and, to them, she probably appears no older than thirty, thirty-five. Ptolema smiles and shows them her middle finger, and they shut the fuck up and mind their breakfasts. Perhaps it was the impatience in her eyes. Maybe they caught sight of all the secrets there, all the necessary evils of her station, all the men and women she's sent to Charon—by her own hand or the obedient hands of her subordinates.

Ptolema stares at the door, as though she can will the Xers to show up.

The coffee steams, and she tries not to think of Deer Isle, Maine. She hasn't entered the quarantine zone herself, and she won't if she can help it. Thank you very much, but there's plenty enough ugliness this side of the pond without going abroad in search of more and better. Let the CDC handle it, the CIA and the NSA and that Other American Group that has no official or unofficial title, those faceless, hollow men who crouch in the shadows beneath an Albany skyscraper and are ever on standby when this sort of shit goes down—which seems to be happening more and more often, and fuck all if she even wants to know why. It's not her *job* to know why. That's way above and beyond her pay grade. It's only her job to monitor the comings and goings of the X. To fathom the unfathomable, as it were, because how do you understand the goals of an organization so secretive 99.9 percent of its operatives have only the faintest idea of the big picture and are let loose to make up the dos and don'ts of a mission or experiment as they go along. Anarchy leaves almost as bad a taste in Ptolema's mouth as would the crap they sell at that McDonald's across the way.

The four German kids depart, surly and still muttering amongst themselves. She checks her watch again—10:45. And she's just about two centimeters away from *Screw these idiots, and screw Barbican* when she catches sight of two faces that match the photos tucked into the dossier in her satchel beneath the table. These expats, supposedly cast out by their own designs. Fallen from their brethren quasi-Buddhist, mongrel Hindu, cyber-Shinto, Gnostic Thelemite worshippers at the shrines of Castaneda, Crowley, Camus, Blavatsky, Robert Anton Wilson, Velikovsky, Berlitz, Charles Fort, ad infinitum, a congregation based, possibly, in Saigon, or Calcutta, or Buenos Aires, or, more likely, nowhere at all. Anyway, this pair of ladies, they look like the rough end of flattened shit. Even more tattered than in their photographs. A wonder someone didn't turn them away at the door, because they sure as fuck look more like panhandlers than anyone who could afford a meal or a pint. Between them, probably not even the €2.20 for a side of potato farl. Oh, but how looks can be deceiving, and for all she knows, these two might be goddamn stockbrokers or solicitors on the bum. Still, no one's going to touch an X. Not anyone who isn't deep in the know. Won't have the foggiest why, so call it instinct. In their rags both genuine or carefully cultivated, these two weave their way between the tables, untouchable because *that's the way it is.* Fucking ghosts, the whole lot of them. Even rogue agents like these two—assuming they actually *are* rogues, and that's not just another layer of some other ghost's one-dimensional logistic map or what have you. Ptolema sits up straighter and straightens the lapels of her leather blazer—force of habit from years when the Y didn't send her out to do business with sketchy cocksuckers, when the Bureau's resources were not stretched so bloody thin, and Ptolema was held back for shadow dignitaries and face-to-face sitdowns with those occupying *unquestionable* power, for whom appearances actually mattered.

They reach her booth, there below Harry Clarke's windows. One of the women is a tall redhead with a buzz cut and a ring in her nose. The other's not so tall, and her black hair's pulled back in two long braids. Right off, it's obvious neither of them are Irish. Ptolema doesn't even have to hear them speak to know that much. Americans, the both of them, and she'd bet half her Swiss bank account on that. They slide into the seat across from her.

"You the Egyptian?" the redhead asks in a phony brogue. "You P?"

"When the need arises," Ptolema replies, "but not in my fucking trousers." And she points at a stain on the crotch of the redhead's jeans.

The girl with the braids laughs. "Cute," she says. "Real cute."

"Told you," says the redhead, "that she'd be like this. Every one of them, they're all cheeky, smart-mouthed cunts."

Ptolema checks her watch again. "I assume tardiness is a point of pride with you."

"Close enough," says the redhead. Beneath her biker jacket, she's wearing an oatmeal-and-mud-colored sweater that might once have been white. The array of buttons festooning the jacket is just a little too deliberate. But only subtly so, not the sort of affectation one would notice unless one were trying to spot affectations, which Ptolema can't help but do. It keeps her on her toes. It's kept her alive more than once. Even the selection of buttons—a red anarchy symbol on a black field, the Sex Pistols, a skull and crossbones, the Dead Kennedys, the Clash—and the array of spikes and studs set into the shoulders and collar and sleeves. It all comes off prefab, calculated, studied.

"Didn't whoever holds your leash bother to inform

you of the current decade?" Ptolema asks and points at the jacket. "The X must be even more desperate than usual."

The one in braids (who isn't wearing a biker jacket, just a ripped-up Bauhaus T-shirt and a ratty faux fur leopard-print coat) leans over and whispers in the redhead's ear. The redhead laughs.

"I'm not going to ask your names, because I neither need nor want to know them," says Ptolema.

"Good, because we weren't planning on tellin' you," the redhead replies.

"Always convenient to be on the same page."

"If you fuckin' say so," shrugs the redhead.

Ptolema removes an early model iPod from the inner pocket of her blazer, complete with earbuds. She sets it on the table between them.

"You've both assured me you're turncoats," she says, "but policy is to treat all defectors and moles as redoubled agents. Ergo, I am proceeding on the assumption that this will, sooner or later, get back to Julia Set."

"We don't parlay with JS no more," says the redhead. "Bridges burned good and fuckin' proper."

"Bureau policy. Not my call. Also, we know the X routinely factors traitors into its equations. Free variables, as it were. But, as I've said, that's our working assumption, and we've taken it into account. Nonetheless, I am instructed to proceed on good faith."

"Which means *you* lot are desperate," smirks the woman with braids, and she reaches for the iPod. "What's this, then?"

Ptolema lets her have it, though she'd intended the redhead to hear the recording first. There's the second deviation from Barbican's itinerary.

"That's reason number one that we're having this conversation," she says. "Our people in Manhattan and Boston are picking it up all over the place. A twenty-four-second transmission broadcasting on pirate stations. On FM, it's popping up at ninety to ninety-one megahertz, and on medium wave exclusively at 1710. We've spotted it on single sideband modulation, as well, and shortwave. And we have five instances thus far of it having been embedded in pop and country songs on several Top 40 FM stations."

The redhead glances suspiciously at Ptolema. "Thought this was about—"

"We'll get to that. But first, we're getting to this. Consider it prologue, okay?" And Ptolema taps the iPod.

"Whatever you say, sister."

The redhead takes the iPod from her companion, so, hey, a smidge of realignment, one less red mark. She puts the buds in her ears and presses her thumb against the click wheel. Immediately, she frowns and shakes her head.

"Just fuckin' static," she mutters.

"That passes. Shut up and listen."

The redhead shuts up, and Ptolema watches her closely. The first tell could come right here, the very first hint the X might be lying. Long, long ago, Ptolema learned to read body language like it was words on a printed page. But the redhead's reactions are genuine. Thirty seconds pass, and she takes out the earbuds and silently stares at the iPod a moment before she says anything. The woman with black braids watches her closely.

"Yeah, well, that is the dog's bollocks of mental, I'll give you that."

Ptolema has a sip of her coffee, gone cold now, then asks the redhead, "Where'd they find you two, anyway? A trailer park in Muskogee, Oklahoma?"

The woman with black braids snickers and elbows her companion.

"So, tell me what you heard," Ptolema says, setting down her cup.

"Nothin' much," the redhead replies. "The static, yeah. Then a little girl, kid's voice. Creepy, innit?"

"What'd she say?" asks black braids.

"Six words. Just six words. 'Black queen white. White queen black.'"

"What the feck does *that* mean?"

The redhead stares at Ptolema, as if waiting for an answer to black braids' question. Instead, she has questions all her own.

"First time you've heard it? Either of you?"

"Sounds like chess shite to me," the redhead mutters.

"Okay, fine, so I'll take that as a yes."

"Take it however you want. That's all you got?"

Ptolema reaches underneath the table for her satchel. The worn leather is camel hide, and there are cracks here and there. She unfastens the strap and removes a manila folder. She lays it on the table next to the iPod.

"The phrase you heard is also turning up as graffiti, but the taggers we've questioned don't know shit about it. Or if they do, they won't say. A week ago, Xeroxed fliers started appearing in both cities, Boston and New York, just those six words, always on canary-yellow paper."

"Canary," says black braids. "Like the bird?"

Ptolema ignores the question, but does note that the woman no longer seems to have an interest in hearing the recording for herself. Which might mean several things or might mean nothing at all. But worth noting, regardless.

"It's nothing from our cell," the redhead says, then glances over her shoulder towards the doors and the big windows fronting Bewley's. "Can't speak for all the others, but you know that."

"Of course," Ptolema tells her. Then she opens the folder, and on top there's a glossy color photo of a woman standing on a street corner. There's nothing especially remarkable about her appearance, and if that's deliberate she's mastered the art of blending in. A little frowzy, maybe. She's wearing a windbreaker the color of an artichoke.

"This was taken here in Dublin three days ago, up on Burgh Quay. I'm not going to ask if you know her, because all three of us already know the answer. She goes by Twisby."

"Yeah," says the redhead, and she doesn't say anything else about the photo. She takes out a cigarette, but doesn't light it. She just holds it between her fingers. Ptolema can see she's getting nervous, but anyone could see that.

"And now this woman," Ptolema says, pushing aside the first photo to reveal a second. The woman in this one is as striking as the first was plain. She's sitting on a park bench reading a paperback. Her white hair is cut in a bob. "I snapped this on St. Stephen's Green yesterday."

"The twins," says black braids and chews at a thumbnail. "The albinos. One of them. Think that's the one calls herself Ivoire. That's her mac, yeah? Always wears that thing, if it's rainin' or not. Yeah, that's Ivy."

"Ivy?"

"Yeah, Ivoire," says the redhead.

"But Ivoire—Ivy—and the Twisby woman, you've never seen the two of them together, have you?"

"No," replies the redhead. "That's not the way it works."

Ptolema sets aside the second photo, and there's one below it that could be the same person. Same face. Same cornsilk hair and haircut, same pale complexion, same startling blue eyes. She's sitting beneath a tree, also reading a paperback. They are, in fact, both reading the same book, which is plain upon close inspection: Kurt Vonnegut's *Cat's Cradle.*

"No. Yeah. That one's the other. Bête, I mean," black braids says around her thumb. "Feckin' bitch, in on what they're doin' to her own sister. Just wrong, by anyone's standards of fair play. Not just her sister, either. But guess you—"

"—already know the twins are also lovers?" interrupts Ptolema. "Yes. We know that. And the two of you have spoken with all three of these individuals?"

"That's why we're here, innit?" asks black braids.

Ptolema returns the photos to the folder, the folder to the satchel, and she fastens the strap again. She returns the iPod to her pocket.

"That all?" asks the redhead.

"No," Ptolema says. "That's us just getting started. But

it's enough for this morning. We'll talk again tomorrow night. I trust you two know Beshoff's, on O'Connell."

The redhead nods. "We know it."

"Eight o'clock. And at least consider being on time, will you?"

The redhead moves the unlit cigarette between her fingers the way a magician might a coin. But then, she is a magician, isn't she? "My associate and I will take it under consideration, guv'ner." She's trying to sound cocky, but she's rattled. That's good.

Ptolema pays them both, even if it's only a formality and she doubts either of them needs the money. Then again, if they aren't lying and they've actually severed ties with Julia Set, they could be poor as fucking church mice.

"Eight. Beshoff's. Don't you keep me waiting again."

They slide out of the booth, one after the other. Before the pair turn to leave, the redhead grins and says, "Like you have a choice."

When they've gone, Ptolema considers going to the counter and getting another cup of coffee, maybe even something to eat. Instead, she keeps her seat and lets her eyes trace the angles and drink in the backlit colors of the stained-glass windows until her phone rings.

2.

Anybody Could Write a True Story

(STONINGTON, MAINE, 9/28/2012)

It's dawn, unless it's sunset. I'm sitting on the mattress, and Sixty-Six is sitting on the other side of the room listening to me. It isn't true to say that she never speaks, but it's true to say that she very rarely ever speaks. I talk enough for the both of us, and if it bothers her she has never said so. Watching the sun rise, or set, I've been talking, this time, about expectation effects, straying into the Gettier problem, propositional knowledge, epistemology, observer-expectancy and subject-expectancy effects. I will not say that she is enduring my rambling patiently or politely because Sixty-Six is not blessed with an overabundance of either of these qualities. I am the nattering; she the hush-hush. Yeah, and then, without warning, she reaches for the rifle on the floor, rises to her knees, rests the gun on the attic windowsill, and fires five shots—*bang, bang, bang, bang, bang*—in quick tattoo succession. I don't have to look to know that she's dropped one or two or several of the demons that have marched out of the sea. *Battalions of the accursed, captained by pallid data that I have exhumed, will march . . . some of them livid and some of them fiery and some of them rotten.* Who wrote that? I cannot remember now. The pain, the dope, the way horror can turn to the mundane, to existential shock, it's all made a sieve of my mind, and now memories slip straight through. You'd never know, Bête, that I was who I was two months ago. You'd never know me, I fear. Sixty-Six lingers a moment at the window, then sets her gun aside and goes back to her place on the floor. She's not unpretty, despite the darkness like bruises that surrounds her oddly golden eyes. Her ebony hair hangs in unkempt dreadlocks, except when she ties it back. Almost always she keeps it tied back, out of her face. (The lead in my pencil breaks, and I have to stop to sharpen it again with my pocketknife.) There are days and nights (though the two are now, here, hardly distinguishable, one from the other) when I fancy her my shaded, sooty twin. But don't think me unfaithful, Bête. The air in the attic is still jangling from the gunfire, but I ask her if she'd like me to stop nattering; she knows it's what happens when I get nervous. And I'm almost always nervous, unless I'm on the street or on the beach and those things are coming at us and I don't have to think about anything but the Ghurka blade in my hand cutting them down. Then I am calm, and the pain fades away, no matter how long it's been since my last fix. Sixty-Six shrugs. She shrugs a lot, but I do try to talk less. I'm getting on my own nerves. Down on West Main, I hear more shots, other soldiers sent here to do no good whatsoever, unless we are actually holding the line and the demons haven't made it off Deer Isle to the mainland. But how is that even possible? We can barricade the bridge and shut down the fishermen and ferries, and the CDC and DOD and agents of X and Y and the Albany spooks can all do their very best, even the endlessly circling patrol boats we have been told keep watch over Eggemoggin Reach and the rest of the bay. We can do all that, but we can't see what's going on below the sea, now can we? Below the surface of the sea. So, I think there are the usual lies, though I try to pretend otherwise. I'm here to do the job I'm here to do, to flap my wings and set distant hurricanes in motion. That's what I'm here to do, to mind *sensitive dependence on initial conditions,* the voyeur of utter destruction as beauty, marking micro-changes in deterministic nonlinear, nonrandom systems. No, no. Not marking them. Setting them in motion. Whatever it was out there Sixty-Six just put down, well, the death or deaths sent ripples, as did the bullets, and her every move during the act, and the weight of the gun on the sill, and my interrupted words and thoughts. And a million other variables that will have so many repercussions to echo down history to come. History of the future, that's what we are making. Maybe the rest are fighting the scourge, but not us. We only *seem* to be soldiers against these interlopers; we are actually instigators, toppling dominoes, setting in motion. "Deterministic Nonperiodic Flow," 1963, *Journal of the Atmospheric Sciences,* 20 (2): 130–141, Dr. Edward Norton Lorenz (also author of the concept of strange attractors, near and dear), an MIT alumnus just like Father. I have written equations on the attic wall, for old times' sake and more for comfort. I've stopped trying to explain them to Sixty-Six, because I'm pretty sure it bores her almost enough to turn that rifle on me. There's no theory in her chaos. She doesn't need theory when she's so adept at the practice. The magic I do not believe in swirls around her, before my very eyes, but I'm not ever again going to believe what I see, and I know that. I sometimes wonder if behind her dirty face and smudgy eyes Sixty-Six harbors an intelligence to put us both to shame, dearest Bête. If she has any other name—and she must—she's never going to let it slip. A time or two, she's whispered this or that about her past, and, by the way, she can't be more than, I don't know, twenty? Twenty-two? Her mother sent her away to . . . a hospital? I'm not sure, but it shows. I check my wristwatch, which tells me that is sunset out there. Well, if watches even work in this event horizon that was once an island off the coast of Maine, notable only for its granite quarries, the Haystack craft school, lobsters, the one-time home of Buckminster Fuller. In *Travels with Charley,* Steinbeck wrote, "One doesn't have to be sensitive to feel the strangeness of Deer Isle." So, how long *has* this place been wrong, and was it always set to be the epicenter for this plague? Was it always damned? Have we—all the shadow people—been sitting back for centuries or millennia waiting for this to begin? Or did a butterfly only recently flap its wings? Sixty-Six is staring at the window and eating from a bag of stale Funyuns. We eat what we can find in what is left of the grocery stores and convenience stores and restaurants. That's not much, but the heroin has mostly killed my appetite anyway, and Sixty-Six, she doesn't seem to mind the slim bill of fare this ruin offers. I believe she could live off candy bars and Skittles. A wonder she has any teeth left. She looks away from the window and says to me, "We should go soon." By which she means, I understand, that if we wait much longer I might miss the drop, my week's supply of dope to keep the agony at arm's length. The pain they gave me so I'll be a good marionette, as if taking you away from me weren't enough. I think it's cancer, but there's no way to know. Not like I can get to a doctor. There were a couple here in Stonington, but they died shortly after the first wave rose up and slithered across the sand and docks and over the seawalls. I got only Vicodin and Percocet at first, then oxycodone, then the heroin. The stations of my walk to addiction to make of me a junkie. Anything to dull the pain. The needle and the blade, because I haven't mentioned (or have I?) that the pain fades completely away—I mean *entirely*—whenever the killing starts. Numbness is my reward for being a good tin soldier, a dutiful agent with initiative, who only rarely receives direct orders, who acts on her own recognizance. And, Bête, here's the rub, I am becoming precisely that, and I mean without worrying about your safety, without the carrot-on-a-stick, without any coercion. I am beginning to feel as though I was almost meant to come here and to be what I have become, these days and this island and Ivoire set on an inevitable intersecting path from the birth of the universe, Planck time, zero to ~10-43 seconds, and there was never any doubt that this is how it would go. Sixty-Six is up, pulling that filthy pink hoodie over her head, reaching for her coat. She tosses me my coat, too. And my pack. So, sorry Bête, that's all for now. *What rough beast slouches* time. Time to fight the thunder and the lightning and the obscuring, suffocating mists that roll in from the wicked, wicked sea.

3.

A Wolf at the Door/It Girl. Rag Doll.

(5/7/2112)

The *Argyle Shoestring* moves listlessly south, and Johnson has spent the past fifteen minutes gazing out a starboard porthole, towards the vast salt marshes cradling the ruins of Old Boston. His grandfather was a meteorologist who served on the Intergovernmental Panel on Climate Change, but, long ago back then, the IPCC's direst predictions never went so high as seven goddamn meters of new ocean by the turn of the century. Surprise, motherfuckers. The air through the open porthole smells of the poisoned sea, and for one who's spent too much of his life cowering among industrial squalor, it's a welcome smell. A comforting smell. Out here, a citizen sailor on a village barge, a man can still be free, or he may at least manage to *pretend* he is still free. All this water is under the jurisdiction of the Far Shore Navy, expanded U.S. territory since a quarter century ago. But, this far north, mostly they have their hands too full up with contraband from the cross-Arctic smugglers out of Russia and the Northern European Union to spare much time for drifters. Ahmed says something, something that he makes sound urgent. Ahmed makes almost everything sound urgent. Johnson closes the brass hatch. The hinges squeak. There's an undeniable melancholy to the skeletal remains of those distant, marsh-bound skyscrapers, only half visible through the haze. Melancholy, but hypnotic, and so it's sort of a relief, whatever Ahmed's on about.

Ahmed is sitting in front of one of the antique QD-LED monitors, data streaming down the screen like amber rain, bathing his face in amber light. Ahmed Andrushchenko is not a man who is well in the head, and lately his periods of lucidity have grown fewer and farther between. But Johnson doesn't mind his company. Plus, the man's obsessions with all the ways history might have gone, but didn't, help to pass empty hours when the comfort of the sea and the village sounds drifting down from above and up from below, the motion of the barge on the waves, are not sufficient. Almost always, he's harmless enough, is Ahmed Andrushchenko, and when he begins drifting towards the bad days, Johnson always manages to keep him from tearing up the cabin they share below the markets. Different rhythms soothe different people, and Ahmed says that Johnson's voice soothes his tattered mind.

"It won't last very long," Johnson says, "before a back-trace snips you."

"Fuck them," barks Ahmed, without daring to take his eyes off the screen. These fleeting uplinks to one or another satellites are too precious to him.

"One day, they'll trail you, and the entire village is gonna lose input and output, all because one man couldn't keep his eyes on the now and tomorrow." Johnson, whose first name is Bartleby, but no one's called him that since he was a boy, sits down in his bunk and sighs. "You can be one selfish prick," he says.

"And *you* can be a nearsighted cunt," Ahmed says.

Johnson shakes his head and stares at the walls of the cabin, decorated with Ahmed's collection of pinned lepidoptera, almost every one of these species extinct fifty years or more. He buys them off the merchant skiffs, or, more often, barters his mechanical and process skills for the butterflies. No questions ever asked, naturally, but Johnson knows most have been looted from the unreclaimed ruins of museums or stolen from other collectors' private vaults.

These butterflies, at least, will never again flap their wings.

Today, Ahmed is chasing the twin, the one who proved dominant, the one who proved the force with which to be reckoned when push came to shove all the world off its foundations. He spends as much time chasing the albino as he spends mulling over the taxonomy of his bugs, picking through conspiracies printed on decades-old buckypages and Teslin sheets. As much time—more, really—than he spends muttering at inattentive Johnson about the Martian refugees and their dead air since the war, or the lights over Africa and Argentina, or the strategic excise bioweapons that are rumored to have been deployed against India when it withdrew from the Global Population Control Initiative two years ago.

"She's here," says Ahmed. "You have to read between the under-code, then filter that through a few archeo El-Gamal and syncryption algorithms, but she's here all over. Shitbirds didn't think she could spin chess, but they were sorely mistaken, my skeptical friend."

"I never said I was a skeptic," Johnson mumbles, no matter how little of Ahmed's absurdities he believes; he says it anyway.

"See, now that's all middle game," Ahmed says and taps on the screen. "You never get much of her middle game. Most of it's sunk too deep in the sats. But, fuck me, this is only '26, and she's already got king safety down to an art. She's hitting the internationals so hard even their material advantages have been pummeled into irrelevance. Oh, she's moving to a very violent position. That strategy is beautiful."

"Give the devil her due," Johnson says.

"Goddamn right."

"Well, be that as it may, you best spool and close it down now, Ahmed. I'm not kidding. I'm the one who'll catch fuck and back if you get the ordinances on us."

"My friend, you ought to see this. I wish you could appreciate—"

"C'mon, Ahmed. I'm not in the mood for this today."

Ahmed's fingers are dancing over the keys fast as a screw from a ten-penny whore, but Johnson's been counting and he knows that Ahmed's gone over the eight-second mark. Johnson might as well be a gust of wind seven miles away.

Ahmed calls out the moves, tongue almost as fast as his fingers.

"42.cxd4+ exd4 43.Kd3 Kb4 44 . . ."

"Okay," Johnson says, getting up, crossing the cabin while Ahmed is still too caught up in the twin's mythical corporate game of chess to see him coming. "I try to play nice, and you know that." Johnson presses the downlink key, and the screen goes a solid wash of amber light. He braces himself for the full fury of Ahmed thwarted. The man's brown eyes are, all at once, choked with anger.

"You don't *do* that, Ahmed," Johnson snarls. "You don't even *think* it. How many teeth you got left you can afford to lose?"

And there's a good argument. But the fire in Ahmed's eyes begins to flicker out, and he just sits there, quietly fuming, staring at the monitor.

"I was getting close," he says disconsolately.

"Yeah, you were. Getting close to buying the whole barge a pudgy good fine." And Johnson pulls the cover down over the cabin's wall unit. Then he goes back to his bunk.

"You think they *don't* want us to think she was never real?" asks Ahmed.

"Who's 'they'?" Johnson asks back, even though he knows the answer perfectly well. This is their own game of chess, the one that these two men play every few days. *Huge sea-wood fed with copper burned green and orange, framed by the coloured stone, in which sad light a carvèd dolphin swam.* Isn't that the way it goes? *"What shall we do tomorrow? What shall we ever do?"*

"They, you idiot. *They.*"

"Don't call me an idiot, Ahmed. I don't like it when you call me an idiot."

"You think I am a lunatic."

Johnson rubs his eyes. He didn't know, until this moment, how tired he was.

"I think you need another route to time displacement, that's all. This ain't healthy. In fact, this is dangerous, cutting into the feeds like that. And Jesus, I'm tired of telling you this. How many times have I told you now?"

"She was a genius," Ahmed says, almost whispering. "But that does not mean someone could not have interceded before she reached middle game."

"Your book says someone did. A whole several someones, if I recall."

Ahmed has two books, actually. Two genuine analog books from the back before: *A Field Guide to Eastern Butterflies* and *The White Queen*.

"I mean to say . . ." But then it's as if he forgets what he's saying, loses his train of thought before the sentence is hardly begun.

"I know what you mean to say, Ahmed. Don't let it eat at you. I know what you mean, so don't worry."

"Here is the day," says Ahmed, and this time he actually is whispering, and Johnson almost doesn't catch the words. Also, just as he says it, the *Argyle Shoestring* takes a rogue wave across her bow and rocks to port, so there's another distraction. But *Here is the day,* that's a folk hand-me-down, a scribble in the margin of paranoia, what some believe were the last words from the twin before the sky went black and the night came crashing down so, so long ago. Read that bit as you will, literally or figuratively.

"Right, well," Johnson tells his cabinmate. "This is what I've heard."

And then Johnson turns back to the porthole glass and watches the sun sinking over the Massachusetts horizon while Ahmed goes to his trunk to get the plastic chess set.

4.

Black Ships Seen Last Year
South of Heaven

(DUBLIN, 13/10/2012)

As an American colleague of Ptolema's has said to her on several occasions, *There is late, and then there is not fucking coming, so give it up and go home.* She's sitting alone picking over the sad remnants of her €7.50 plate of smoked cod and chips. Her mouth tastes of beer, malt vinegar, and fried fish. She pokes at the rind of a lemon slice with her fork, then her eyes wander once more to the tall windows facing out onto Upper O'Connell Street. No sign of either the anonymous redhead or black braids. She knows their names, of course, all of it right there in the dossier, and, sure, they know that she knows, but this is how the game is played. She stops stabbing at the lemon slice and pushes the plate away. Late was an hour ago.

Maybe, maybe, she thinks, *I should ditch them both. They're playing me, or they think they are. It's all a goddamn puppet show for the X. It's never much of anything else from X, now is it?*

She finishes the dregs of her second pint of the evening and briefly considers ordering a third Guinness. But her head's already a hint of cloudy, and it's not completely beyond reason to suppose that the pair, or one or the other of them, might yet turn up. So, no more alcohol. When she gets back to the hotel, she'll turn to the bottle of Connemara and let the whiskey do its job good and proper.

Enough is goddamn enough, she thinks. *No one can blame me for canceling on a tête-à-tête that's never coming. I'll call Barrymore and lay it all out, start to finish, and, if I'm lucky, he'll tell me to take the next plane the fuck out of Ireland.* She leaves a generous tip, then abandons the warm sanctuary of the restaurant and steps out into the raw and windy night. Ptolema buttons her coat and turns up the collar against the cold. She follows O'Connell Street south and crosses the bridge, then stands at the edge of Aston Quay, watching the dark waters of the peaty Liffey sliding past on their way to the sea. She folds up the collar of her coat and winds her scarf more tightly about her face. This wind'll strip the skin right off your bones, and here it is not even November yet. The freezing air smells like the river. It smells like the algae clinging to the constricting stone channel through which the river flows. On the opposite shore, back the way she's come, Eden Quay is a garish spray of neon signs.

Ptolema isn't aware the redhead is standing only a couple of feet away until the woman speaks. "I'd say I'm sorry about being late," she says. "Only I'm not, and I'm not in the mood for lies, if you catch my drift."

"You might have let me know." Ptolema unwinds the scarf from her face, so her voice won't be muffled by wool. The redhead has dropped the phony accent, so at least there's that.

"Might have, but I did not. Bury the past. Move on. Keep on truckin'. Here we are now, and now we can conduct our business beyond the attentions of any we desire not to know our business."

"You think I don't have other problems besides you?" Ptolema asks her. "You think you're at the very fucking top of my list of priorities?"

"I do," the woman says, and she lights a cigarette. She exhales smoke and the fog of her breath. "At the very tippy top, or near enough. I thought you wanted me to drop all the deceits, Miss P."

"So, we're going to stand out here in the cold and have this conversation? I'm going to placate you and freeze my ass off because you're afraid someone might overhear us in a fish-and-chips shop?"

"If you actually want to hear whatever it is I have to say. I know you Y sorts. I know if there's one of you, then there's two, and I know if there's two, there's four. I'm keen to your exponential support protocol."

"Our what? You just fucking made that up."

The redhead takes another drag on her cigarette and shrugs.

"Are you here to listen, Miss P, or are you here to talk?"

Ptolema takes a punt Éireannach from a pocket and tosses it into the Liffey, a shiny red deer cast in nickel and copper for goddesses forgotten or goddesses who never were.

That there, that's not me—I go where I please—I walk through walls, I float down the Liffey . . . In a little while, I'll be gone. I'll be gone. I'll be gone. Must then my fortune be . . . wake by the trumpet's sound . . . and see the flaming skies. I'll be gone.

Her random thoughts, that come and go, talking of Michelangelo.

O O O O that Shakespeherian Rag.

"Fine," Ptolema tells the redhead. "Twisby and the twin, the twin named Bête."

"You don't like what I got to say, if you think I'm bull-shittin' you, you got orders, don't you? Terminate. Terminate, with extreme prejudice, just like Jerry Ziesmer tells Martin Sheen in *Apocalypse Now.* That's how it is, I know."

Ptolema chews at her chapped lower lip, smothering impatience.

"And we shall play a game of chess?" the redhead asks her and laughs.

"No more games. No more stalling."

"But what about your recording, Miss P? Your creepy child's voice from out the ether. Is it not commanding that we do just that?"

Ptolema wonders how many years or centuries the coin will lie lost among the rocks and silt on the riverbed. After even she's dead. Long after this crisis has come and gone and is only an ugly shred of occult history. The X would build an entire equation around the consequences of her having tossed a punt into the river.

"Twisby and the twin," she says and leaves no room in her voice for any more nonsense from the redhead.

"Like the Bard himself done said, as you like it," she replies. "Yeah, I saw 'em both. I talked with 'em both, but that's the part you already know, and fuck all if I dare waste your precious time."

"This was after you met Ivoire."

"You know that, too. Yeah, it was after, down at Kehoe's pub, but you also already know that. So, fast forward. Total cunt of a day, and mostly I was just wanting to get drunk, but I have friends who hang out there, so I was hoping to see them. Two birds, one stone. But that night, none of them showed, which was a bummer—"

"I'm not here to discuss your social life. Twisby and the twin."

"Jesus fuck, lady. I'm getting to them, okay?"

The October wind is a wailing phantom through the bare limbs of the few skinny trees lined up along the quay. Ptolema shivers at the sound, though she knows perfectly well there's nothing the least bit ominous about it. There's nothing at work but her exasperation, exhaustion, and imagination. Nothing but the reports and rumors from Maine. That, and this Twisby person and the twins to set her nerves on edge.

A red deer on a coin.

Cervus elaphus scoticus.

Deer Isle.

Odocoileus virginianus.

The Commissioner has warned her time and again not to let it get inside her head, that miasma, the muddling aura that surrounds every last agent of the X. But Ptolema knows it's exactly what she's done. The redhead is talking; Ptolema curses and wonders how much she's missed in the lapse.

" . . . not the same shade as mine, but more like an auburn. Tied back. She wasn't drinking anything, and she hardly said one word the whole time. It was mostly the twin, mostly this Bête girl said what was said. It wasn't all that much, mind you, but it was enough. Frankly, more than I wanted to hear, seeing as how Ivoire and I were already close enough to friends. Well, as close as you get to making friends these days, right?"

Ptolema quit smoking nearly fifteen years ago, but she almost asks the redhead for a cigarette. She's still shivering and tries to stop. It's a sign of weakness, and you never let an Xer see that kind of shit. They drink it up like nectar.

"I can't recite it word for word, but the gist of it was Bête *knows* it was someone on our side made her sister sick, someone on our side set up this whole masquerade about her sister having been kidnapped. Put it in Ivoire's head—brainwashing, menticide, thought reform, hypnosis, don't ask me—that she'd lend her not inconsiderable talents to the cause and march off to that unholy fucking shitstorm in Maine, or else her sister would be tortured, raped, ravaged, tagged and bagged, whatever. That it was the X sending Ivy the goods."

"The drugs?" Ptolema asks her, and the redhead nods.

"Ivoire, she told me it was just pills at first, but that wasn't enough. The pain was way beyond vikes and percs, you know. And, from what she said, it was like whoever was in back of this operation knew that, which is when the heroin started coming, instead."

"But Ivoire's never seen who delivers the packages?"

"Nope. They just show up. Sitting on a fence post with her name written neatly on the brown paper wrapping. Or tucked into a knothole in a tree she just happens to pass. Shit like that. Happenstance. But every time she's running low, the deliveries show up like clockwork. Tick tock."

"And now it's heroin."

"Yeah. Not as if she had any say in that. She told me when they cut off the oxy, she scoured the whole god-damned island, top to bottom. But after the looting and the fires, wasn't nothing left. Piddley-shit, one-whore place only had, what? Two drugstores to start with. Fuck it."

Ptolema rubs her hands together. The gloves aren't helping at all. If the cold bothers the redhead, she's doing a good job of pretending it doesn't.

"And her sister knows all of this? Bête?"

"Miss P, I'm pretty certain that's what I just said. We've ... they've ... got her buyin' into that whole util-itarian, greater-good crapola. Hook, line, sinker. There's her sister out there, her fucking *lover,* sick as a dog and probably dying, and now she's a junkie, and there's hardly ever a moment she doesn't seem terrified about what's happening to Bête, but Bête, this Twisby woman has her full fucking cooperation, wrapped around her pinkie fin-ger. Nothing's going too far."

Ptolema stops rubbing her hands together—it's point-less anyway—and she says, "This can't be the first time you've seen them pull this level of shit on someone." The redhead is quiet. She doesn't answer the question that, to be fair, wasn't really a question. She doesn't say whether she has or hasn't seen this sort of shit before. Which, Ptolema knows, means that of course she has. It's de rigueur, business as usual in the trenches of an invisible war that's never had honor or a code of conduct or a Geneva Convention and never fucking will.

"Go on," Ptolema says.

"That sounds an awful lot like an order to me," says the redhead.

Ptolema rubs at her eyes. They feel as if they're turning to ice. "Sorry. I honestly didn't mean it to," she says.

"You watch that tone, then. Where was I?"

"Twisby appears to be controlling Bête, and somehow they're both controlling Ivoire."

"Right, so at first the Bête twin, she was all puffed up, pleased with herself and these sick machinations, pure, undiluted braggadocio. But then she mentions someone called Sixty-Six, apparently another good lil' factotum shipped off to the Pine Tree State. That was about the first time Twisby perked up. Shot Bête this ugly stare, reproach, you know. Disapproval. But not like it was a secret that Bête shouldn't have let slip.

More like Twisby is carrying a beef of some sort with this Sixty-Six. More like that. Maybe. I don't know."

Ptolema stops rubbing her eyes. She's afraid they might shatter if she keeps it up, the way a rose dipped in liquid nitrogen shatters when struck against a hard surface.

"You know who this Sixty-Six character is?" she asks the redhead.

"I got some intel. Not a lot, 'cause her profile is buried in lockdown. But I fished up some tidbits. She was deployed shortly before Ivy. They met afterwards. Sixty-Six's not much older than the twins. Twenty-ish, so about the same age as the twins. She spent some time in a mental hospital in upstate New York. Her parents had her committed when she was just a kid. But, out of the goodness of its heart, JS sprung her."

"You know why?"

The redhead looks annoyed, shakes her head, and flicks the butt of her cigarette at the river. A trail of embers follows it down.

"How the hell would I know a thing like that? I'm sure there was some reason deemed sufficient and necessary to keep everything moving smoothly as shit through a goose."

"Okay, so Twisby doesn't like Sixty-Six."

"Not if that glare meant anything. But after she gave

Thing Number Two that nasty look, Bête's whole demeanor changed. You'd have thought someone flipped a light switch in her soul. So, right off, seems to me Twisby has Bête on a short tether. But, as I said, this twin gets all twitchy, flinching, not half so talkative. Went virtually catatonic, then and there. I'm not ashamed to admit, gave me the willies even more than I had them already. That's when the taciturn Doc Twisby begins speaking directly—"

"Doc? Twisby's a doctor?"

The redhead mumbles something Ptolema can't make out over the wind.

"I strongly dislike being interrupted," the redhead says, and she fishes another cigarette from a pocket and lights it. "Almost as much as I dislike taking orders."

Ptolema apologizes.

"I figured that much out just watchin' her, yeah. But afterwards I tapped a contact of mine at Cal State, and yes, she is a doctor. Neurology. Biopsych. Oxford and Yale alumnus. High profile in the APA. But then, plop, she drops off the academic radar, only to pop up on *another* radar. Three years, she was cryptologic, No Such Agency, Never Say Anything, black ops, clandestine research feces had her bouncing back and forth between the NSA and Homeland Security and OSIR. Mostly OSIR. Some highly weird goings-on, from what I was told. She—"

"How did your contact learn anything at all? If

'Twisby' is only her alias—"

"Two strikes, lady. Three, you're out, and I'll take my chances with your wrath."

This time, Ptolema doesn't bother apologizing. The redhead continues.

"*As I was saying,* if you will please fucking recall, Madam Doc Twisby was up to something unpleasant with covert funding from these various sources, shadow phenomenology bushwa, way above top secret. I'm guessing, obviously, some manner of next-gen weaponizing."

"It's better if you refrain from guessing," Ptolema says. The lights across the Liffey have her thinking of a carnival now. The redhead is silent long enough that Ptolema has begun to believe she's not going to get anything else out of her, when the woman starts talking again.

"We . . . they . . . pulled her. Not sure when, but, near as I can suss, no one in Washington raised a hand to prevent her departure. Even for the X, that's kind of ballsy, dipping into TPTB's talent pool with such complete confidence. Which sets me thinking there's an arrangement in place, tit for tat, an exchange of information in the offing. Naturally, those fucks in the States won't get anything but a stingy fraction of whatever comes of Twisby's mouse-in-a-maze experiment. Whether or not they know this, bugger all if I can tell you."

"Okay," Ptolema says, when she's sure she isn't interrupting the redhead. Sure, she has orders to kill her. But she doesn't want it to come to that. Not just yet, not with an informant who could still prove valuable further down the line. Not just yet. This could, of course, change in a matter of seconds, with a phone call, a text, the tip of a fucking hat. "We have a former high-profile psychiatric wiz using these two twins for fuck only knows what. Julia Set has Ivoire—reluctant soldier—convinced her sister will be killed unless she follows orders, and, as added insurance, extra control, they've infected or poisoned her, turned her into an addict, and have her dependent upon them for heroin. Have you considered she might only *think* she's sick?"

"I have," the redhead replies. "But, way I see it, pain is pain."

"Her twin," Ptolema continues, "with whom she's been involved in an incestuous relationship for seven years, since the two were thirteen, not only has no problem with this, she's helping out." Ptolema is suddenly, and, she thinks, unaccountably seized with a need to lean over the rail and vomit her dinner and all that beer into the river.

"Sorry about that," the redhead says. "The nausea will pass. Probably. My focus has never been spot on. Chaos can be goddamn chaotic and all."

"Fuck you," Ptolema mutters and tries to concentrate, but she can taste bile. "After your confab with these two sweethearts, did either of them say they'd be in touch again?"

"Nope. She did not."

"She?"

"Doc Twisby. Got hostile there at the end. I ought to mention that. Stopped just short of making full-on, out-and-out threats. But close enough the hairs on the back of my neck were prickling. Sufficient tension in the air I was wondering if I could reach the Glock in my shoulder holster before she pulled some sort of telekinetic nonsense or what have you. Pyro- or cryokinesis. Quantum tunneling. Doesn't matter if you wind up on the wrong end of the stick, now does it?"

"She's TK?"

"That's the vibe I got. Same with Thing Number Two, and, I'd bet a hundred large, same with Ivy."

Ptolema pinches her septum, hard enough her eyes water, because sometimes that helps when she's motion-sick. And whatever inadvertent energy has sloughed off the redhead and onto her feels more like motion sickness than anything else.

"But she didn't do shit. Little staring match there between me and the Doc, and Bête doing some sort of origami shit with a bar napkin. Oh, hey, I haven't mentioned that, have I. See, the twin, she kept making origami swans. They looked top notch to me, but every time Twisby would shake her head and Bête would get all hangdog and start over. Fuck me in the ear if I know what *that* was all about. By the way, Miss P, is it true the twins are some sort of prodigies? Geology, some sort of something of the sort?"

"Evolutionary biology," Ptolema replies. The nose-pinching remedy has done no good whatsoever, and her stomach rolls. "Paleontology. They were both grad students before this began."

"So we've a crop of brainiacs all round, don't we. Yeah, Ivy dropped hints to that effect. But I don't always know what's crap and what's for true. Though, here's what I still don't get. Why is it you lot are chasing after this Twisby and her pale riders? Or is that need-to-know?"

Ptolema shuts her eyes, then opens them again. She truly is going to puke. And it comes to her this isn't an accident. This is the redhead's safety net, just in case the meeting goes sideways and she needs an exit strategy. "You heard the recording," she says quietly, and swallows.

"'Black queen white, white queen black,'" says the redhead, sounding amused. "You don't look so hot there, Miss P. Gone a little green around the gills. But, the recording. Gotta admit, don't see how it hooks up with the twins."

"Then you're dumber than I've given you credit for. Think. Ivoire and Bête?"

"Yeah, and?"

"Ivory beast," says Ptolema. She knows that it's only a matter of seconds now until she loses her battle with the nausea.

"*Damn,* yeah. Dude, how did I *not* see that? White queen. Two white queens. *Dangerous* white queens. So, you're thinkin' the message refers to those two? You know, if the gods send worms, that would be kind, if we were robins."

"And just what the hell does *that*—" But Ptolema doesn't finish. Instead, she rushes to the railing and hurls into the Liffey. And when the cramps and dry heaves finally pass, there's no sign whatsoever of the redhead. She may as well have been a ghost. A hallucination. A false memory.

5.

How Ghosts Affect Relationships

It is everything but an understatement to call this room white. It is white in so absolute a sense that it is almost impossible for the eye to detect the intersection of angles where the four walls meet ceiling, where ceiling meets walls, where walls meet floor, to pick out each individual object placed within the room, for all of these are completely white, as well. The furnishings are few and plain: a bed, a nightstand, a white lamp with a white lampshade, a blank white canvas within a white frame, a white table and two white chairs—one placed at the north end of the table and one at the south. On the southern wall, there is a window, one window with white drapes. Outside, snow is falling so hard the land and sky blur together, whiteout conditions. The white door with its white marble knob is set into the eastern wall. However, any sense of direction would be lost as soon as one were to dare enter the white room. Indeed, even the ability to tell up from down would be jeopardized. *That* is how achromatic is this room.

Though Lizbeth Margeride has no recollection of ever once having entered the room, she has been here many, many times, and, in its way, each time has been different. But always her awareness of being here begins with her seated in the white chair at the southern end of the table, facing her sister, Elle, who sits at the northern end, facing her. Both of them are wearing nothing but white camiknickers that would have been fashionable in the 1930s, with matching white stockings and Mary Janes. There is a chessboard on the table between them, and it, too, is entirely white, every one of the sixty-four squares precisely identical and yet unmistakably distinct.

The first violation of the room's immaculateness is the sixteen and sixteen chess pieces themselves, as there are both white and black pieces. The black pieces are arranged before Lizbeth, and the white before Elle. It is appropriate, Lizbeth thinks, as Lizbeth always thinks, that her sister will make the opening move, as is ever the privilege of white, in keeping with the color scheme of the white room.

The second violation is the sisters themselves. Though their hair and eyebrows are almost as pale as the room, their milky skin seems just shy of pink in this place, and their blue eyes are as radiant as star sapphires. Their twenty fingernails have been polished crimson. Their lips are rouged. Shocking dabs of color amid the tyranny of white.

White.

This is the illusion of a single "color" perceived by the three sorts of cone cells present in the human eye when confronted simultaneously with all the wavelengths of the visible spectrum at once. White isn't the absence of color, as many mistakenly believe. It is, rather, the perfect reflection and perception of all colors, therefore the *antithesis* of black—black being perfect absorption, which is the perception of the absence of color.

Elle moves her queen's white knight ahead two spaces and one space west.

Lizbeth studies the move. It may seem hours before she counters.

One must move with the utmost care.

Too much is always at stake.

Always.

Sometimes, even the gods themselves are merely pieces in a higher game, and the players of this game, in turn, are merely pieces in an endless hierarchy of larger chessboards.

"My move," Lizbeth says.

"Take all the time you need, love," answers Elle, as she always does. "What matter if you take a hundred years?"

She speaks with neither malice nor restlessness.

"A slow sort of country," said the Queen. *"Now, here, you see, it takes all the running you can do, to keep in the same place. If you want to get somewhere else, you must run at least twice as fast as that."*

Beyond the white door lies an endless white hallway. Lizbeth knows this instinctually, though she has never once stood, crossed the room, and dared to open the door. There is a soft horror in all this white that would be increased a hundredfold, she suspects, if the door were ever opened.

I don't really think it's a hallway at all.

It's a maze.

The white hands of the white clock on the white wall count off the seconds, minutes, and hours. There is too much time here, and there is no time at all. In all this white, Lizbeth's thoughts inevitably begin to blur, which is unfair, as one needs clarity for chess, and her sister always gets the first move, being always white, and so still has clarity before the onset of the blur. *This room is,* Lizbeth thinks, *a cathedral to . . .*

To what? Closed systems where entropy prevails? A permutation of the second law of thermodynamics? Quantum mechanical zero-point energy? Dissolution? The Nernst heat theorem?

Insanity?

Faultless sanity?

"If you're cold, love," Elle says to her, "you may open the window."

I may, yes. No one and nothing is stopping me.

Then comes the third violation. Her name is not Twisby, but that's the only name she has ever provided the twins. Or her name is not Thisby. There is sometimes contention between the sisters on this point, but the woman has never offered a definitive answer, no matter how many times they've inquired. *She is someone we will meet.* Lizbeth knows that, just as she knows that her first move will involve a pawn, no matter how much she wishes otherwise. She knows that the woman is threat and shelter, peril and deliverance. A future catalyst. When the woman speaks, the air shimmers and the twins turn towards her in unison. The legs of their white chairs scrape, in unison, as a single sound, against the white floor.

"There is but one evil," the woman named Twisby (or Thisby) tells them. "Only a single sin. It is waste. Were it not for me and what I will teach you when you are ready, you would be wasted. I cannot abide that. I will come to light the fuse. To provide the push that will be necessary to begin the—" She pauses, then adds, "To begin the cascade."

The woman opens her hands. Her left palm has been

painted as red as the twin's lips and fingernails. Her right is the color of Lizbeth's chess pieces, which is to say *all* colors.

"Quietness is wholeness at the center of stillness," says Twisby (or Thisby). "But this is only your cocoon, Lizbeth. This is only your cocoon, Elle. Such a metamorphosis awaits you. You will see. There will be no waste. No sin. No evil."

And then she's gone.

"Your move," says Elle.

"Yes," replies Lizbeth. "My move."

When at last she wakes from the dream of the white room, Lizbeth Margeride lies very still, smelling her own sweat on the damp sheets, and she keeps her eyes trained on her sister, still fast asleep in her own bed. She watches Elle until dreams come again.

6.

Late Saturday Night Motel Signal

Well, baby, I came here for more than *that.* I've seen self-disembowelings, the ballet of now-time Americanized sep-púku, hara-kiri, performance-nuanced 腹切り dazzling in scarlet river splendor. I cover the war, as is the battle cry in these nether ditches of secrecy that all are meant to see, as many as will watch. Cryptic voyeurism, right, bitcast for the world if it bothers to look or glances in by accident. Now, *that,* I think and always have thought, must be the cat's velvet paw: *Überraschung,* mothercocksucker! Looking for peeptalk line telly, a bit of footsy ball or hoops, and here's this bitch over there on the bed turning herself inside out. But yeah, no. I ain't taken this job and come to this shitty Chinatown flop for no floor show. My motives are, shall we say, ulterior. I'm here for the other thing. I'm chasing a ghost. Her names, she has so very many now—like mind tattoos or identity memes ladled by the fans—all of which run irrelevant to my purpose.

I am assuming I have anything as concrete *as* a purpose.

See here, all of this web been spun from out a dream I cannot stop having, an echo's echo coughed up from my scorch-fed back brain, 404-transcription break-down between my dear and darling hippocampus and neocortex, expectation fulfillment retro-slip out activation-synthesis. Sara White Queen of auld lang syne, how she collected dreams in blue-bottle skull-fuck yottabyte quantum cat boxes. SWQ Check, do love such like REM of serotonin and histamine reflux. Now, how-some-ever, is she gone away across the grey Atlantic to Londontown and left me all alone. We are both drawn to our half-drowned burgs, and I could clip the sleeping phantasies across the satellite hand-offs to her, sure. But I won't. I might let some snick whore suck me off standing right the fuck here in Room 707, but my subconscious sick, that's not for any brigand flensing the sky who just happens across them in hisherit's driftnet by-catch. I want her to have them, I'll hand deliver.

I digress.

I did spend some days and nights down Atlanta way. This was before those homebrew prepper Hitler fetishists popped off the CDC containment protocol and the city went what it is today. This was in The Day, back in, and I am during these rapid repeater dreams towered high above the Midtown rabble, in a room always different from *this* room tonight. Wait, no, yes. That's how I meant to couch that. I am there in a suite I never could in all my squalid lives pony up, but I am there, regardless, and the Woman in White, Lady of the Many Names, there is she, as well. Down in the guts, covering the war, you hear tell of the WiW, though she's a tripper urban legendary lady, not what you put your eyes and hands upon. But for a happenstance few only a necessary fiction to be exploited by the blippers. Still, there she is, sparklesome as December tinsel treeforms, and she says, and I gaze out at the neon sodium-arc headlight mercury vapor OLED thoroughfares like Jesus in his high place of temptation. And she says, I said, and what exactly does it matter the precise of her words? *She* says them, and she says them to *me*. And mallet to the meat, that is. The air outside the vast window is swarmed of a sudden with flittering crowblack wings, raven eyes, a vortex of feather beats upon the twilight. She says, though it might have been any, but let's set down some arbitrate specificity, she says the names of Not Gods and all their not-holy retinues in turn. Dapper scar, you bet. Cuts my throat in essence, those immemorial words that could spell The Over Ending if there's any truth *in* her book.

Well, let me not here do the untruthful pitter-pat. Not *her* book, at least in my dream it's not her book. It is, no, rather, hauled from out the sea, and she says hauled from out the sea off the coast of Massachusetts, twixt Boston and Provincetown. Except other times, when says hauled from the Sea of Maine. She sits tidy in a comfy big damn chair, smoking and reading to me from the undrowned volume. Oh, I haven't, no, not have I asked to hear the gospel long written down, but that don't stop her. She is a big spun herself gossamer off the cuff, as they say of her in Old New Amsterdam. A being of her own devising, and that includes not soliciting the opinions of those to whom she evangelizes.

Lo, whiche sleighets and subtilitees . . .

Our all-media suicide du jour accepts from her jisatsu second the nightly's highstand tantō. The suicide is dressed in hooker's lace and gild, which says so much and hardly anything else at all. This is how they would have her, the penitentses, the gawking predynastic underdogs, the slavering, and the casually curious got the best of them. She both gazes into the camera's eye and the camera gazes from her own complex optical system, her twin gelatin vitreous seas. Before this night, she was fitted with the host's pricey implants so it flows both ways, receive and transmit, because who does not want a good and for all of the faces of the audience she has called from every cranny and nook and penthouse shitter? Myself, covering the war, all I need for the job of work has been seen to by the network engineers and underling sawbones. She grips the samurai knife tightly in both hands, hilt bedward, blade to the low popcorn ceiling. Mind wandering, as I am not here to see that, I wouldn't wonder if that ceiling were sprayed in place all the way back in the nineteen ands. I'm chatting up the live feed with my shifting thoughts, and a producer whose name I can't recall, she reminds me I promised her to keep off my come-natural street shanty. I tell her she can two-second delay and run it through the translators. She says a bad word, and then, well, she says a few more.

The woman on the bed has jellybean hair.

Indeed, without an oathwhich, bewept on a cheap duvet, gives me superfluous death, O how the wheel becomes it. Got that, studio? Got that? Thought and afflictions, hell itself? Heel, then, head over?

I was speaking of the dream, digress reminisce, and of the Woman in White, as she inhabits that dreamtime, when it comes to me again and again and again. The woman on the bed, she'll wait, I am sure. Not goin' nowhere. And, remember, I am *not* cum for her. The hostess here in 707 passes me a beer, though in the dream my throat and mouth go parched. But, no, yes, in her chair, chain-smoking, there is the WiW, who is no older, they say, than that day on Deer Isle—you believe that part, and if you credit a sliver might as well credit the lot for a penny, for a pound. Her face stops clocks, as they say, her heart going tick-tock-tick-tock-tick-tock-tick-tock, and she stops me, too, with that beauty. She actually is talking about tranporteichon, and I tells her I takes the bus. I likes the bus. Gives a fucker time to think. Then she returns to talk of assembly programs, authoring systems, naked-eye constellations, transistors, protoplanetary party-time. I turn away from the mirror, and she smiles, oh *god* does she smile for me. Eyes as blue as Howlin' Wolf. She sees my reaction and offers me a couple of slickers, a bebop, and one of her contraband Czech cigs. I accept the first, and I accept the latter. I dry swallow and ask her for a light.

"*That's a neat trick,*" I say.

She shrugs.

"*Mr. Carlisle, what was it you wished to discuss?*" she asks.

Wait. What? Dreaming, that's my inline thought, because I have shit-all recollection of desiring to talk about anything at all.

She smiles again (unless it's that still same smile from before), says, "Je suis sérieuse et j'écoute attentivement."

I almost remark how I dream French better than I speak or understand it.

"*True you're Queen Bee?*" I ask.

Again with the thwarting shrug.

"*In Cleveland, I heard the tape,*" I tell her, and awake I

will admit that's a lie. They keep it wrapped, the buggers, and I've only laid my ears upon the thirdhand whisper dubs, iymk.

One of the crows does as good as that woman on the 707 bed and nosedives into the sheet glass behind me. Pow. I jump, but the WiW does not so much as flinch. Like they tell, ice water in her veins. She's chili swag, Arthur.

"Do you play?" she wants to know.

"Chess?"

"Chess," says she to me. *"Of course, chess."*

"No."

On the bed in 707, meanwhile back in the now awake, achy-achy shake-and-bake, I do believe the suicide is bracing for the first cut. I hold to and appreciate this timeworn tatterdemalion ceremony, more than the more fatter of mac routes to death. Those make shit telly, someone drinks drain cleaner or takes a load of pills. And guns are just lazy. Oh, but this once, up in Beantown, I filmed one of these soirees whence a girl swallowed liquid nitrogen. You shoulda seen that one. The ratings went to the moon, three times around, before the referees in legal found a microscopic wrinkle in her contract and shut down the feed.

In her chair by the ATL room's only and one lamp, the alabaster Queen Bee shuts her eyes a moment. I know well enough she's jetlagged. I know that, dreaming the way we dost tumble to things not would we know *not* dreaming. I try not to stare at the tip-jab-coddles all down her left arm. In the dream, she's on the needle, but down in Atlanta, who isn't, yeah? No? Though, she ain't from Atlanta, just passing through, and just passing through, apparently, because I wanted to talk with her.

She opens her eyes, and then another bird hits the window.

"Last month, was that you on the waves? Or was that your sister?"

Rumor has it about the sister, though R&D swears sis is still more mythic than the WiW herself. But I cover the war, and that makes gold of rumor and only copper or antique green paper of whatever the nerdulent crowd back in the tower have to say. The producers understand that, sometimes.

"Je ne suis pas venue ici pour discuter ma soeur."

Oh, so she's feeding me run-through Franco now, *so* possibly she believes I chat only that low gutter punch. I'm not insulted, just . . . ya know.

"You've never discussed her with anyone," I say, immediately wishing I'd not.

"You're not even watching her," someone says through my ear. *"What do you think we're paying you for, Mr. Carlisle? The bed, Carlisle. Keep your eyes on the damn bed."*

"Fuck you," I mutter, 'cause they peg a mutter as clearly

as a shout, but I dutifully redirect my head to the woman on the bed and her shiny knife. She must not have had enough preparatory sedation, because the lady's looking scaredy.

Dapper scar, indeed.

7.

The Way Out Is Through

It was almost an hour past dark by the time we made it back to the attic. I can only be sure of the transition by recourse to my watch. In its current condition, the sky is hardly a help. So late in the day, we shouldn't have been that far from the attic, not so far as the docks at the end of Seabreeze Avenue. But we needed food. I'm sick as a sick dog today. The pain has been a hammer pounding my entire body, glass and razors in my joints and lungs and belly, but I didn't dare fix until we got back here to sanctuary. The dope is as good as any toxin out there in the turmoil at the end of the world, which is to say it will get you killed. Sixty-Six hates when I call this that, *the End of the World*. She never says so, but she makes the face she makes whenever she disapproves of something I've said. I think of it as her Disapproving Face. Anyway, I fixed almost an hour ago, and now there's only the music of Hell seeping in through the walls and the open window. Never mind the season; tonight it is too warm to shut the window. Still, despite the heat, Sixty-Six keeps her hoodie on. I've stripped down to my bra and panties, and I'm still sweating. Drips of me, of my internal ocean, splashing against the dusty floor as I write this. *My* ocean is clear, though, not the sloshing putrescence of the bay, of all the sea surrounding Deer Isle. We found a tidy cache of food in the harbormaster's office—cans of meat and vegetables, mostly. We filled our packs, and it should keep us fed a week, at least. *If* we live another week. Sixty-Six seems indifferent to survival, and, at times, fuck but I wish I were, too. Then there would only be the monotonous rhythm of pain and the freedom from pain the dope brings, the heroin's euphoria, our days on the street hunting down the demons (I do not mean this word in any conventional sense; no other seems to fit, that's all), gunfire, the hilt of my holy *khukuri* in my hand, slashing the air, slashing flesh that isn't flesh. Matter, protoplasm, *Urschleim,* but not flesh. The stink of ozone when I have no choice but to resort to those intangible weapons folded up inside me. The howling, capering abominations. But we're home again, "home" again. Me and taciturn Sixty-Six. There's a crooked stack of books beside her mattress. She reads. She reads as much as I did, before. We found the public library our first week here, not long after we found each other, and it was one of the few instances when she's seemed happy. She used a shopping cart to haul away dozens of books. Now, I think they keep her company much more than I do. *They* are her solace. I want to talk about what we saw down there this afternoon, how we found ourselves hemmed in and almost did not make it back. But that is the one subject I can rest assured Sixty-Six will never discuss: whatever's happening here. The sea is the color of semen. The sea is the consistency of jizz. *The scrotum-tightening sea.* It smells like sewage. It steams and disgorges demons. "Demons," with scare quotes. All but shapeless shapes that burst when shot or cut, their constituent molecules thereafter slithering back into the semen sea to reassemble and gather themselves for a new assault. Sixty-Six calls them *shoggoths,* a word she's taken from old horror stories, turns out. I don't care what the fuck they are. They pop and slither off. There's a pretty picture drawn nice as nice can be, isn't it, Bête? I spend my days hoping you are safe, that they are doing you no harm. I spend my days in slaughter, in a charade meant to convince the few survivors in Stonington that we have their irrelevant interests at stake. That we are more than two lost souls, refugees ourselves, sent here to topple the dominoes just so, perpetuating calculated chaos, perhaps for no other reason than because curious men and women desire to see the pretty fractals that will follow from our efforts. Last night, Sixty-Six was reading *The House at Pooh Corner,* and since she doesn't seem to mind my talking while she reads (so long as I don't expect replies), I rattled on for a while about Tuscaloosa and mine and your time at the university. Oh, she did find it odd that we chose to go to school in Alabama, when she knows (I do not know how) that we might have had our pick of the Ivy Leagues. Anyway, yes, I talked about fossils—how we were the first to find the blastoid *Granatocrinus granulatus* in the Fort Payne Chert; how, as undergraduates, we named *Selmasaurus russelli,* a new genus and species of *plioplatecarpine mosasaur*; the papers we delivered together on mosasaur biostratigraphy at annual meetings of the Society of Vertebrate Paleontology (Ottawa, Austin, Cleveland, then Bristol and our first trip to England); taking part in the dig that produced the tyrannosauroid *Appalachiosaurus,* our small role in some of the preliminary examination of the skeleton while it was still in the matrix and plaster field jackets; the mess with FHSM VP-13910, how *we* prepared it and first saw it for what it was, a second specimen of *Selmasaurus,* but the credit going to others and all our work and insight left unacknowledged; collecting Oligocene fossils in the White River Badlands of Nebraska; standing in the wooded gully at Haddonfield, New Jersey, where, in 1858, the first American dinosaur known from more than a few scraps was discovered; how we were the first to happen upon and describe the remains of a velociraptorine theropod from the Gulf Coast (even if it was only a single, tiny tooth). I went on and on like that—*Ditomopyge,* Carboniferous chondrichthyans, *Globidens alabamaensis,* the Pierre Shale at Red Bird and Pottsville Formation at Morris, that skull of *Megalonyx jeffersonii* we prepared but were afraid we'd screw up and so didn't finish (one of many failures, I admitted), freezing strip mines in the winter and blistering quarries and chalk washes in July... and on and on and on. She *heard,* but I'm pretty sure she didn't *listen* to a word of it. She is a master of compartmentalization. Anyhow, I don't care what William Faulkner said, Bête. I think the past is the past, for us, and we can recall those days, but we'll never go back to that life we cherished. Will we. No. Science and reason are being demolished around me. Paradigms are being reduced to matchsticks, to splinters. Incommensurable topsy-turvy. I hope you are safe, sister, and that they are keeping their promises. I'm doing everything I'm told. To the letter. I am obedient. But that's always come easily to me. Not like you, sweet Bête. But I know even if I do not die here, if we ever are reunited, there is no going back. Now, returning to the matter of the Semen Sea, here is what we think we know, pieced together from hearsay, frightened confessions, newspaper and other local periodical accounts printed in the weeks before it began (*Commercial Fisheries News, Compass Classifieds, The Deer Isle Chronicle, Island Ad-Vantages,* et al.) from captains' logs we've recovered off derelict fishing boats: On the night of August 20, a chartreuse light fell screaming from the sky. It is agreed the light did scream, or whatever cast the light screamed, as it fell into the bay somewhere beyond Burnt Cove. But the sun and the stars were still visible until the twenty-seventh, when the visibility zero-zero began rolling in *from the east,* so not from the direction of Burnt Cove. Empty boats, dead fishermen found floating or washed up to make a feast for crabs and gulls and maggots. The greasy rains and the sickness that came after them, the plague that killed more than 78 percent of Deer Isle's population before we arrived, the whatever-it-was the CDC couldn't even slow down before it claimed most of their team, too. The stars coming back ... wrong; unrecognizable, alien constellations spinning overhead. Yes, I do sound like a madwoman, and I don't expect any of this will ever be made public. If it is contained, if it ever ends—The Event—they'll be sure no one talks, I think, even if it means murdering everyone who survives. There will be a mock-rational explanation. Mock science everyone will want to believe, because believing the truth—even were it not concealed—would be intolerable. But enough for now. Sixty-Six has dog-eared a page and put her book away. She wants me to turn off the Coleman lantern. I need the sleep. Tomorrow will be at least as bad as today, as bad as yesterday, as bad as day after tomorrow. Or worse. Night, sister. Sweet dreams.

8.

Golgotha Tenement Blues/Counting Zeroes

(11/15/1966)

Wait. Let's not get ahead of ourselves. Shun a premature narrative, lacking necessary background exposition. Ergo, the future, which will shortly be spoken of as the past, the *future* of the past (as all futures are), 1973 and the inter-governmental hysteria rightly triggered by the indiscretions at the Watergate Hotel. The steps hastily taken to destroy records of *previous* indiscretions, and among them the efforts of CIA Director Richard Helms to annihilate all evidence of Project MKUltra. Between the early 1950s and 1973, the CIA's secret efforts at behavioral engineering in humans. This fell to the members of the Scientific Intelligence Division, who dutifully employed "chemical, biological, and radiological" agents to accomplish their ends, along with a buffet of torture, sexual abuse, sensory deprivation, prolonged verbal assaults, and so forth.

LSD was popular.

Had Helms been successful, MKUltra would have managed to disappear. No mean feat, that would have been. But spooks are notoriously fine magicians. Only, Helms was the cut-rate sort of magician who makes a living at children's birthday parties. That is, if we evaluate him solely on his failure to erase the two-plus decades of *this* project.

Now. Then. Before.

Here is a woman named Madeline Noble. One day, she, unwed, will have a child who will be named Patricia Elenore. In time, Patricia Elenore, at age twenty, also unwed, will give birth to a daughter to be christened Olivia Estrid "Sixty-Six" Noble.

Link to link to link.

Dot to dot to dot.

LSD, amphetamines, barbiturates, ergine, temazepam, psilocybin, mescaline, heroin, 3,4-methylenedioxy-*N*-methylamphetamine, et alia. And the researchers were especially proud of their superhallucinogenic glycolate anticholinergic, dubbed "BZ." Words that roll off the tongue like pretty pharmacological poetry. In 1964, Madeline Noble enrolled at Bowling Green State University, undecided on her course of study, though, ironically, leaning towards psychology. Madeline was one of five students unknowingly administered multiple doses of BZ via cafeteria food. Seven doses, over fourteen weeks, culminating in a psychotic breakdown. Solid data for the studious number-crunchers and keepers of albino lab rats to mull over. Control the mind, control the will. Control the soul. Render malleable strategic individuals, armies, the populous of an entire city malleable or insensible. Whichever equals useful.

That upon the wings of a super-bat, he broods over this earth and over other worlds, perhaps deriving something from them: hovers on wings, or winglike appendages, or planes that are hundreds of miles from tip to tip—a super-evil thing that is exploiting us.

By Evil I mean that which makes us useful.

Madeline. Here she is, in a white, white padded cell, kept safe from herself, in the sense that she may not now do herself bodily harm, may not end the unfolding nightmare of her life. The hurricane within her amygdala, its inability to imagine an end to the storm and send an all-clear to the medial prefrontal cortex. This cyclone puts the anticyclonic Great Red Spot of Jupiter to shame. She is divorced from this place and this time, thrown forward, backwards, and she watches the sky fall whenever she shuts her eyes.

Catch a falling star and put it in your pocket.
Never let it fade away.
Catch a falling star and put it in your pocket.

Save it for a rainy day.

In every way, Madeline Noble is a success story for the geeks and bureaucrats of MKUltra. She is a shining star, falling or not. Hard work pays off and has been rewarded with manna from Heaven, as it were.

As she is.

In her head, the sky falls. There, behind her eyes, it bleeds over the waters of Penobscot Bay, above and upon Deer Isle, where her parents have a summer home. Where she spent her summer vacations, before college. When she is visited by psychiatrists from McGill University, happily serving their CIA manipulators, when they question her for voice recordings and meticulous notes, she recites blasphemies written down and published more than four decades earlier, though none of them will ever make the connection with *his* damned book. How the brilliant are often blind.

They press the record button, pencils held at the ready, ears perked like alert hounds, and sometimes she will sing for them: "When You Wish Upon a Star," "Stars Fell on Alabama," "Catch a Falling Star," "I Only Have Eyes for You." They scribble, and *she* says:

"A thing the size of the Brooklyn Bridge. It's alive in outer space."

"Something that big? Wouldn't we have seen it?"

"*Shhhh,* Logan. Don't interrupt her."

Madeline is silent for a moment, glaring at the three men in her cell. And then, again, she says, "A thing the size of the Brooklyn Bridge. It's alive in outer space.

"Something the size of Central Park kills it.

"It drips."

"Jesus." Logan whistles to himself.

"Showers of blood," she says. "Might as well *be* blood. One especial thing, a thing the size of the Brooklyn Bridge, as there are vast living things in the oceans, there are vast living things in the sky. Leviathans. Fleets of Leviathans. Our whole solar system is a living organism, and showers of blood are its internal hemorrhages." There are no italics here because every word she says is emphatic.

"Rivers of blood that vein albuminous seas."

"Dreiser, how do you spell 'albuminous'?"

"The phosphorescent gleam seemed to glide along flat on the surface of the sea, no light being visible in the air above the water. Though . . . disruption may intensify into incandescence, apart from disruption and its probable fieriness, these things that enter this earth's atmosphere have about them a cold light which would not, like light from molten matter, be instantly quenched by water. They still burn. They can't stop burning."

She names asteroids that have not yet been discovered.

She describes, in great detail, Saturn's north polar

hexagon, which will not be observed until the year 2005.

She also describes Io's volcano Tvashtar, the frozen seas of Europa, the September 18, 2006, discovery of a supernova 240 million light years away.

She asks them, "Who are the twins?"

She asks, "Who is the Egyptian? Who is the Wandering Jew? Have you any idea how long she's been alive?"

She asks, "What is the ivory beast?"

"What is the meaning of 'black queen white, white queen black'?"

And after a prolonged silence, followed by a fit of laughter that not a man among her watchers does not find disconcerting, she turns her head towards the ceiling. And taking great care to enunciate each syllable so that they will not mistake these words for any others, she says, "Gentlemen, we have arrived at the oneness of allness. A single cosmic flow you would label disorder, unreality, inequilibrium, ugliness, discord, inconsistency."

"Jesus *Christ*," Logan mutters. "Haven't we heard enough of this foolishness for one goddamn day?"

"Don't make me tell you to shut up again."

"Checkmate," says Madeline. "Because this is the meaning: Black queen white, white queen black. A game of chess played in the temples of Eris, the halls of Discordia. There will be murders on *la manzana de la discordia*. You know, or may learn of, Omar Khayyam Ravenhurst, not his real name, but let that slide. The gods were not pleased, and so, of course, all were turned into birds. Even the birds will rain down upon the bay and upon the island. Eris tosses the golden apple, and the sea heaves up her judgment upon us all. Watch for the Egyptian and the arrival of the twins and my daughter's daughter. Watch for Strife, who, warns Homer, is relentless. She is the sister and companion of murderous Ares, she who is only a little thing at the first, but thereafter grows until she strides on the earth with her head striking heaven. She then hurls down bitterness equally between both sides as she walks through the onslaught, making men's pain heavier.

"The calla lilies are in bloom again. Such a strange flower—suitable to any occasion.

"Be still," she says. "The chaos rains around you now."

She tells them very many things, and these things Richard Helms *will* succeed in expunging from the knowledge of man. In that, at least, he will be successful. There are those *outside* the CIA who will see to that.

Later, on the flight back to Montreal, Dr. Allan Logan examines their notes. "Thank fuck we know that woman will never have a daughter, much fucking less a granddaughter. Whatever Washington is aiming for, I believe they overshot the mark with that one."

"Ours is but to do or die," replies Dr. Dreiser.

"That's not how it goes."

"Not how *what* goes?"

"That poem. 'The Charge of the Light Brigade.' Tennyson. It goes, 'Theirs not to reason why, theirs but to do *and* die.'"

"Fuck you, Logan." With that, Dr. Dreiser shuts his eyes and concentrates on the rumble of the Boeing 707's turbocompressors. He dislikes air travel almost as much as he dislikes Logan.

But a daughter *will* be born to Madeline Noble.

And a daughter to *her* daughter.

Eris plays a mean game of chess.

9.

Bury Magnets. Swallow the Rapture.

(17 VRISHIKA, 2152)

She sits on a bench in the main observation tier of the
Nautilus-IV, her eyes on the wide bay window set into the
belly of the station, the icy spiral of the Martian northern pole filling her view. *She* being the White Woman. *La
femme albinos. Ca-ng bái de. Blancanieves.* More appellations hung on her than all the words for god, some say.
But if she has a true name—and doesn't everyone?—it is
her secret and hers alone. A scrap of knowledge forever
lost to humanity. So, her blue *eyes* are fixed on the
Planum Boreum four hundred kilometers below, yes, but
her *mind* is on the Egyptian—Ancient of Days, el Judío
Errante, Kundry, Ptolema—she has many names, as well.
The Sino LDTC ferrying her is now less than eight sols
out. The Egyptian racing towards her. An unforeseen inconvenience. In no way at all a calamity, no, but still an
unfortunate occurrence to force the White Woman's

hand. It tries her patience, and patience has been the key for so long that she cannot even recall a time before she learned that lesson.

In less than eight sols, the transfer vessel will dock, and they will speak for the first time in . . .

Ça a duré combien de temps?

She answers the question aloud: "Cent trente-neuf ans."

"Vraiment?" asks Babbit. "Autant que ça?"

When she arrived on the station two months ago, Babbit was assigned the task of seeing to her every need. As has been her wish, he hardly ever leaves her side. The company of anyone is a balm for her sometimes crippling monophobia. A medicine better than any she has ever been prescribed. It doesn't matter that this tall, thin, tow-headed man is only mostly human. Many times, she's resorted to and relied upon the companionship of splices. Besides, Babbit's fast borrow capabilities saved her the trouble of telling him all the tales he needs to know to carry on useful conversations. And there will be much less fuss when she orders his death, before her flight back to Earth. Easy come, easy go.

"Vous n'êtes jamais allé à Manhattan," she says.

"Madame, c'était perdu avant que je sois né."

"Ah," she replies, and the White Woman holds up her right hand, absentmindedly running fingertips along the window, tracing the serpentine furrow on the Chasma Boreale. It seems almost as long as her long life, and almost as aimless. *Possédé de direction,* she thinks, *être dirigé n'est pas la même chose que de diriger.*

"En tout cas," she says to Babbit, "nous étions à Manhattan. Je venais de rentrer de la Suède. Il y a si longtemps. Presque de retour au début."

"Autant que ça," he says again.

"Je ne pourrais pas commencer à comprendre ce qu'elle espère accomplir en venant ici et en me poursuivent de cette façon."

"Moi non plus, Madame."

"Il est possible que le vaisseau soit armé. Ça serait bien son style: une attaque préventive, sacrifier le poste entier et tout l'équipage afin d'accomplir ses objectifs."

"Ces fanatiques sont extrêmement dangereux," says Babbit.

"Il n'est pas possible qu'elle espère *raisonner* avec moi. Elle ne peut pas supposer l'idée que nous partageons le même concept de Raison." "Des vrais croyants, je veux dire," Babbit says.

"Je sais ce que vous vouliez dire."

"Bien sûr, Madame."

"Peut-être elle ne souhaite que d'être témoin," the White Woman says. "Être présente quand le cavalier de mon roi prend son dernier fou."

Babbit clears his throat. "Je m'attends à ce que le capitaine ait prévu la possibilité d'une attaque," he says, then clears his throat once more.

She laughs. "Il n'a rien fait de la sorte. Il n'y a pas eu d'alerte, pas de préparation pour intercepter ou protéger. Il reste assis et attend, lui, comme un petit animal peureux qui se recroqueville aux sous-bois."

"Je ne faisais que de supposer," admits Babbit.

The White Woman pulls her hand back from the window, and she seems to stare at it for a few seconds. As if in wonder, maybe. Or as if, perhaps, it's been soiled somehow. Then she turns her head and watches Babbit. He lowers his head; he never meets her gaze.

"J'ai considéré retenir le lancement jusqu'à ce qu'elle embarque," she says to him. "Jusqu'à ce qu'elle soit assez proche."

"Alors vous avez pris votre décision? Le lancement, je veux dire."

"J'ai pris cette décision avant de quitter Xichang. Ce n'était qu'une question de l'heure."

"Et maintenant l'avez-vous décidé?"

No one on the *Nautilus-IV,* no one back on Earth, no one in the scattered, hardscrabble colonies below, none of them know why she is here. Few enough know that she *is* here. She was listed on no passenger manifest. They do not know she's ready to call the Egyptian's gambit and move her king's knight. To cast a stone on the still waters. Not one of them knows the nature of her cargo. No one but Babbit, and he won't talk.

"Maintenant, je l'ai décidé," she tells him, and the White Woman shuts her blue eyes and pictures the vial in its plasma-lock cradle, hidden inside a shipment of hardware and foodstuffs bound for Sharonov. The kinetic gravity bomb will detonate at five hundred feet, and the contents of the vial will be aerosolized. The sky will rain corruption, and the corruption will take root in the dome's cisterns and reservoirs.

לענה

Wormwood.

Apsinthion.

. . . and a great star fell from heaven, blazing like a torch . . .

"Madame," says Babbit, not daring to raise his head. "Êtes-vous sûre d'obtenir les résultats desirés? Il y a des règles d'évacuation, des procédures de confinement environnemental—"

. . . the waters became wormwood . . .

Voici le jour.

"Babbit, toute ma vie je n'ai jamais été sûre de rien. Ce qui en est la cause."

She turns back to the window and can almost feel the wild katabatic winds scouring the glaciers and canyons.

The White Woman pulls her robes more tightly about herself. She's glad that Babbit is with her. She wants to ask him if he might take for granted that she has never loved, if no one has ever been dear to her. But she doesn't.

Instead, she says again, "Ce qui en est en cause."

"Oui, Madame," he says. "Bien sûr."

10.

A Plague of Snakes, Turned to Stone

(*STONINGTON, MAINE, 11/4/2012*)

It is difficult to believe this can continue much longer. The seasons are not changing. It seems as though it will always now be late summer, earliest autumn, here in Stonington, as though this horror has frozen time. And yet we move through time, and we speak, and our thoughts occur, and all that which bears a vague resemblance to day and all that which bears a vague resemblance to night comes and goes. We get hungry. We run out of ammunition. We kill. We forage. All these factors assure me there must continue to, at the least, exist some *facsimile* of time. It's like a forgery by an unskilled counterfeiter. God makes a copy, but he gets it wrong. Or, he gets it different. *The world I have known is lost in shadow.* That shit from the sea, it warps time. Invokes a time dilation that exists between here and, possibly, all the rest of the world. Or—if not a gravitational time dilation, not us beyond the perimeter of a Schwarzschild radius where time comes to a grinding halt on the singularity of a collapsed, frozen star, then a subjective time dilation, happening in my mind. Have I written that already, on some other page? Does it matter if I have? *And the stars are black and cold. As I stare into the void.* Tonight is tonight, and I sat down and opened my notebook and took up my pen to write about tonight. Today, tonight. Both. About how they have been peculiarly quiet. That happens sometimes, the quiet days. The lulls. In a way, they're worse than the day-to-day war we are not here waging upon foes we have not come to defeat. Not in the strictest sense. No. Not the way the few remaining survivors of Deer Isle are fighting. The way the military and the CDC are fighting. You, Bête, you will know what it is I mean. And the pain, it's getting so much worse. There are days now when Sixty-Six has to venture out alone. She never seems to resent my inability to accompany her. Is she relieved? Would she rather do her work alone? Can't say, haven't asked, won't even hazard a guess. Stepping outside today, slinking from our attic because we needed to restock our provisions, because somewhere another domino needed toppling to a faraway effect, we left the attic and realized at once it would be a Quiet Day. I walked along behind Sixty-Six, keeping up as best I can despite the pain in my legs and stomach. She found two

cans of Heinz baked beans and a can of brown bread
in the looted shell of the Fisherman's Friend restaurant
on Atlantic Avenue. This is very close to the public library, and she'd stopped for a couple of new books. We
sat at the end of one of the wharves and ate. She read and
ate. I only ate and watched the sticky sea, which was so
still today that it seemed almost to have solidified. How
and why do I force myself to observe those waters, bereft
of so much as even the suggestion of waves? I do not
know, Bête, my love. The tides do not rise and fall here
any longer, so the horror holds a greater sway than does
the moon. Up there where the constellations shift about,
might be there is no longer a moon, or never *was* a moon.
Consider that! But, we sat together, eating. Me, chewing
but not tasting. Just grinding my jaws. Her reading *David
Copperfield,* between plastic sporkfuls of baked beans. (*I
had considered how the things that never happen are often
as much realities to us, in their effects, as those that are accomplished.*) There was a cramp, an especially bad one,
and I vomited everything I'd swallowed into the sea. No.
Onto the sea. My puke spattered across that pearly surface and lay there. Not sinking. I think it's alive. Have I
said that? That I think what the bay has become is alive? I
wiped my mouth and stared up at the resilient buttermilk
August-September-in-November sky. *We had the sky, up
there, all speckled with stars, and we used to lay on our backs*

and look up at them, and discuss about whether they was made, or only just happened. Sixty-Six turned a page. She did not seem to notice I'd been sick, but I am sick a lot. Old hat. Like bullets and blades and blood and ichor. We no longer find the remarkable at all remarkable. The outrageous is made mundane. I wiped my mouth and said, very softly, "What out there do you miss? Do you miss anything at all?" She continued reading, not raising her eyes from the novel. "What *would* I miss? No." I wiped my mouth again and spat. "Where did you learn to shoot?" I asked, and I admit I was talking just to hear my voice. The world here grows more silent every day. "Nowhere," she replied. She told me how she'd never held a gun before the X came to her and sent her here. "What was there to learn?" she asked. "It's all mathematics. Nothing but a sort of trigonometry." For no reason I can now recall, I then recalled that it was Thursday. On Thursday nights there are films in the National Guard armory. Sixty-Six likes to go. Mostly they screen—yeah, Bête, this part is bizarre—these fucked-up old Disney cartoons, Donald fucking Duck in the army, in World War II. *The Vanishing Private*; there's the only title I remember. Jesus, I'm making less sense than usual, but I had to use more of the dope than usual to so much as sit up and hold the pen. Maybe *you* know why my being made sick is necessary to this experiment—if that is the word—but it is lost on me. Back to the wharf. Sixty-Six set her empty can aside, and I asked if she was going to the movies tonight. She shrugged. All of this was playing out through the fog of pain and drugs dream-like. I don't question that sensation anymore. I reached into a pocket of my jacket, the variegated camouflage one I took from the aforementioned armory (no one tries to stop me from doing anything, not here). A small ammonite like the one you wear on the silver chain around your neck, sister. My tiny black *Hildoceras bifrons* from our trip to Whitby. I held it out to her, its whorl shining dully in my palm. She set her book down and stared at it, seeming truly and totally mystified. "Why?" she wanted to know. Suspicious. "I don't know. I want you to have it, that's all. Maybe because you keep saving my life out here." She took it; I hadn't thought she would. "People don't give me things," she said. "Well, I just did," I said. "You miss things," she said. "You miss what you had before, you and your sister. Your science. The fossils." Practically a sermon, that many words from Sixty-Six all at once. It actually made me smile. "Yeah, I do. I miss Bête, and I miss what we did." Sixty-Six let the ammonite tumble from one hand to the other. "Not just the sex," she said. "Not just the sex," I replied. "I see what you read online," Sixty-Six said to me. (Have I mentioned that, sometimes, the internet is still accessible from the island? Just now and then. One of the terminals in the city hall hasn't been smashed, and I've sat and used it a few times.) "You want to go back." "Don't you?" "Back to what?" There was a long silence then. I heard sirens off towards town proper. I don't know why they still bother with those, but the sound was a welcome interruption on a Quiet Day. "Okay," I said. And then I talked about the last thing I'd read online. Others might have been scouring the web for news of the outside world and whether it has any fucking idea what's happening here. I don't. Last time (and Sixty-Six was with me, searching through old file cabinets, though I cannot say for what) I read *PLoS One* and an article on a recently discovered freshwater mosasaur from Hungary, *Pannoniasaurus inexpectatus,* and sitting on the wharf I explained to Sixty-Six that paleontologists hadn't thought that mosasaurs lived in freshwater. Only, here's the thing, Bête. You'll not have read this article, I don't think. Because *this* was the December 19, 2012, issue of *PLoS One.* And we're back at time dilation. "Look at this," Sixty-Six said, and that she was talking so much, it was starting to freak me out. "Look at this," and she pointed at the little ammonite in her hand. At the center of its whorl. "It begins *here,* and it goes round and round and round, and it's always growing larger from the center. What begins as a point becomes very wide before it ends." I didn't know what to say, so I didn't say anything at all. She understands the heart of it, doesn't she? Every minute action, or omission of an action; every breath we breathe; the shedding of every dead skin cell; every trigger pulled; every man and woman on this island who crosses our path—it all echoes through eternity, growing larger and larger in its consequences as the whorl goes round and round about. Oh, oh. What did I just write? I should not have, should have kept that bottled. I ought to *destroy* this page. I ought to *burn* it and swallow the ashes. Don't follow me, Bête. Whatever happens, don't follow me. *Fais que ton rêve soit plus long que la nuit.*

11.

Throwing a Donner Party at Sea

(5/13/2114)

Today is Friday, though for many aboard the village barges scattered about the globe, and so on the *Argyle Shoestring*, the distinctions between days and weeks and months tend to blur. But not for Ahmed Andrushchenko, who obsessively marks off each date on calendars he makes himself. Bartleby Johnson has never seen the point of it. Sure, the tier farmers and hydroponics need to know the growing seasons, and there are still those who celebrate Christmas, Ramadan, Easter, Chanukah, all the host of High Holy Days, Boxing Day, Launch Day, goddamn May Day, and St. bloody Valentine's Day. There is that peculiarly nostalgic minority. Johnson, he figures it's the norm ashore, that the terrestrials rejoice as a matter of course. But it's raw on the waves, and most old ways have been set aside for the monotony of the deep. Today is Friday, and he's repairing the aft solar-sail array.

It's tedious work—especially with such jerry-rigged replacement parts—but it beats to hell and back passing the afternoon with Ahmed. His latest tiresome obsession is the trans-Neptunian object 90377 Sedna, which by his calculations (and century-old astronomical charts) has recently overtaken the dwarf planet Eris as the farthest known celestial body orbiting the sun. That, and news of the civil unrest in the Greater Republic of India.

Better, thinks Johnson, *that I spend however many hours dangling from this catwalk, suspended above the abyss with a wrench and spanner.*

He is undeniably fond of Ahmed. They've been quarter mates for eight years now, ever since Johnson came aboard in Portugal. But the prattle wears on one's nerves and wears thin. So, times like this he is grateful to be a mechanic, frequently called out to keep this ramshackle cobble-together from breaking apart to scatter across the waves and send them all to the drowning.

Johnson is replacing a shot rivet at the base of the heliogyro when the sirens sound, warning that another vessel is coming alongside. He uses both feet to shove off the hull, swinging his harnesses around for a better view. It's an FS Navy ship, a high-speed trimaran wearing the name *Silver Girl.* Never a good sign, when the Navy bothers sending a trimaran this far from littoral. A voice booms from the *Silver Girl*'s loudspeakers, notifying the barge that it will be boarded in five minutes and to ready the ramp right quick. Johnson curses, takes a firm hold of the crisscross network of safety lines, and hauls himself back up onto the widowmaker. By the time he's unbuckled, navigated the jibboom and bowsprit, then climbed down to red tier, through his spyglass, across two hundred yards, he can see the Navy men are filing onto the barge, two abreast, armed so that it will be obvious to everyone in the village that they mean business. This isn't some sort of routine inspection (not that they'd ever send a littoral trimaran for an inspection).

It might be that crate of black market quinoa, flax, and soy they bartered for a while back. Or it might be the two fugitives they (very unwisely) gave sanctuary down on the Houston wharves, on a Texas run six months ago. Or it might be . . .

Ahmed.

Johnson shoulders through the throng of worried, frightened, and curious onlookers blocking his way. He moves as quickly as he possibly can, and once there's almost a scuffle when he overturns a melon cart. But by the time he's made it to the front of the crowd, one of the Navy men has hauled Ahmed from belowdecks and is leading him in cuffs towards the ramp. Ahmed's head is down, and he doesn't see Johnson. They take Ahmed Andrushchenko away, and not once is there eye contact between him and Johnson. Two midshipmen in hard-shell hazmat suits are carrying Ahmed's footlocker with as much care as they would handle a nuke. A major reads off the charges to anyone who cares to hear them, and before half an hour has passed the *Silver Girl* is rapidly putting distance between them, tacking westward towards shore. In another fifteen minutes, it's only a glint on the horizon.

On his way back to his quarters, Johnson is intercepted by another mechanic—a hulking Scotsman named Galbraith—who wants to know what the fuck *that* was all about.

"He was *your* bunkmate, yeah? Figure you gotta have a notion, yeah? What was in that fucknut's footlocker?"

Johnson shakes his head, and he tells Galbraith, "No idea. His business was his own. But you swim quicktime, you can ask 'im for yourself, yeah?"

"You are a lying cocksucker!" the Scotsman shouts after him.

Yes, I am. Yes, I most surely am. But so are we all.

Ahmed traded a box of chips and circuits for the trunk almost a year back, so long ago now that Johnson can't even recall the name of the barge he found it on. But he does remember the contents. Nothing he'd conjured on overly long, and, truth told, he'd not ever thought of the trunk in quite a while. But now, now, now it was fresh in his mind as that busted rivet on the sail. Mostly there'd only been an assortment of musty old books, a case of roundabouts no machine on a dump like the *Argyle Shoestring* would ever be able to spin, and an assortment of motion cubes—equally fucking useless. Among the books was a volume on advanced chess tactics and another on cosmological inflation theory, and Johnson, at first, had assumed those were the reason Ahmed had bothered haggling for the lot. Until he'd pulled a shiny lead cylinder from the jumble. There was a Category A UN 2814 biohazard designation pressed into one side and also into the lid of the cylinder, along with an MGRS coordinate and date: 19TEJ2629389058—18/2/13.

"No," Johnson had told him, grabbing for the cylinder, no matter how it was scaring him shitless. "That goes right the fuck overboard."

"Screw you, Bartleby," Ahmed said. "It's mine. It cost dear, and it is mine." There had ensued a tussle that ended in Johnson sporting a newly chipped incisor and Ahmed an eye that would go black and blue as storm clouds. But Johnson had given up. He threatened to report Ahmed to the selectmen, but that hadn't made any difference. He threatened never again to play chess with Ahmed, and, again, no dice. Johnson sat on the floor below the porthole, sweating and teasing the damaged tooth with the tip of his tongue.

"You ain't gonna open that, you crazy son of a bitch. Even you're not that daft."

But then Ahmed did pop the seal. There was an audible hiss and a subsequent series of clicks as the cylinder released the inner capsule. A fog of liquid oxygen or nitrogen billowed from the violated artifact, and when it cleared Johnson saw what had been shut away more than one hundred and one years: clamped firmly in place between steel rods, a glowing tube, maybe thirty-five, maybe forty milliliters. Whatever was in the tube had a pearlescent quality about it, and it glowed ever so slightly in the twilight filling up the cabin.

"You got no inkling what that shit is," Johnson said.

"Isn't that the marvel of it?"

"I ought to murder you in your sleep, you bastard. Slit your throat, toss that shit overboard myself." Johnson hadn't meant it, but he was frightened, and his tooth hurt, and he has always been apt to blurt such threats in the heat of the moment.

Ahmed shrugged. "If you gotta, then you gotta," he said, and gazed in wonder at the pearly tube before shutting and sealing the cylinder again.

So, thinks Johnson, sitting on the edge of his bunk, *so somehow the military got word and came for it. Might be they've been doggin' that can around for tens and tens, and Ahmed gets it, and they get Ahmed. Fuck. Fuck. Fuck.*

"*Fuck.*"

That's when Johnson happens to glance at the shelf that holds Ahmed's books, and right off he notices one, and only one, is missing. *The White Queen.*

"Fuck us all," he whispers and lies down and stares at the underside of Ahmed's bunk. Soon enough, it'll be someone else's bunk.

12

If I Should Fall from Grace with God

(BORRISOKANE, COUNTY TIPPERARY, 18/10/2012)

The air inside the safehouse stinks of mildew and stale to-bacco smoke, of Indian takeaway and pine-scented disinfec-tant. Of failure and desperation and of waiting. And, above all, uncertainty. Once upon a time, the shabby little two-room cottage on the outskirts of Borrisokane was an IRA safehouse, sheltering Nationalist fugitives from the North, fleeing the bloody consequences of their patriotic chores. It was not quite so shabby back then. The walls inside the cottage are whitewashed brick and stone, whitewash gone grey from soot and mold and neglect. The floor is bare con-crete with only a few filthy throw rugs tossed about here and there. There's electricity, but no running water, and the roof leaks when it rains, which means the roof leaks quite frequently. There are two portable space heaters that make no difference whatsoever—but it's the thought that counts. There's a room with two cots. There's a hot plate and a kettle, a mini-fridge, a few pots and pans. There's a table crowded with computer and surveillance equipment, sheltered by a yellow polyester tarpaulin. There's a crucifix hung on one wall, like a grudging concession to history. There's a fireplace no one ever uses anymore. There are windows, but they've all been discreetly painted over.

The assassin's name is Nora Swann—at least, that's the name she's worn for the past seven years—and this is where she's been hiding since the great cock-up in Dublin three days ago. This is where her wounds were treated, and this is where she's being debriefed. When she was a younger woman, she worked exclusively for the CIA—in West Berlin, mostly. At her chosen trade she believed herself to be the best of the best, an unquestioned artist with a rifle and scope. But her ambitions led her farther down the rabbit hole, so to speak, and now she's pushing fifty, and Nora serves Albany and the men in black suits and tinfoil hats who answer to no one.

Nora Swann sits on a metal folding chair and squints through her own cigarette smoke at the images projected onto one of the whitewashed walls—CCTV footage from all those days ago, the Dublin fruit and vegetable market fronting Mary's Lane and St. Michan's Street, that vast shed of Victorian stone and ironwork, glazed brick and terra-cotta archways, vaulted skylights to let the unreliable Irish sun shine down on the stalls and the customers and the sellers of onions and tulips. Her thoughts are muddy from pain and from the painkillers, and her stomach is sour from antibiotics and bitter black coffee.

"Nora, we're going to go over it again," says the well-dressed woman who has flown all the way from America to question her and try and make sense of this mess.

"How many times will this make now?" asks Nora Swann, not expecting an answer, and then she blows smoke at the images projected on the wall.

"Do you actually think that matters?" asks the woman from Albany.

"No," replies Nora Swann. "No, of course not."

On the wall, Dubliners peruse seemingly endless rows of cabbages and leeks, apples and pears, roses and calla lilies. Men with hand trucks trundle by, hauling wooden produce crates stacked six or seven high. Merchants talk among themselves or with their customers. It's any market day. It is nothing remarkable, whatsoever. The sight of it triggers in the assassin the memory of the smell of the place, the chilly autumnal air heavy with the commingled odors of growing things. She forces herself not to look away.

"How many weapons were you carrying that day?" asks the well-dressed woman.

"Only the one," Nora Swann tells her.

"And that one was?"

"Same as last time I answered this question, and same as

all the times before that. The Glock 17 nine-millimeter, fitted with an external suppressor."

"That morning, had you suffered any unusual symptoms prior to the encounter, any discomforts? Headaches, nausea, vertigo, a persistent ringing in the ears, any peculiar tastes or smells, anything at all of that sort?"

"No, not before. I was fine before. Before, I was right as rain."

"And you're quite sure about that?"

"Yes, I'm quite sure about that."

"Were you wearing gloves?" asks the well-dressed woman.

"Yes, I was wearing gloves," answers Nora Swann. "Black kidskin over latex. Same as always." She takes a last drag off the cigarette, then leans over and stubs it out against one leg of the metal folding chair. She drops the butt onto the concrete floor at her feet. The cigarettes she's been smoking since she arrived at the safehouse in Borrisokane aren't her brand, and she doesn't like the taste they leave in her mouth, but they're better than having nothing at all.

The projected image changes angle, switches to video recorded by a different camera mounted in a different location within the market. And there she is, splashed across the wall, just another Monday a.m. shopper. Nothing to see here, not after more than two decades spent learning to blend in, learning not to stand out or draw attention to herself. When it comes to mimicry, chameleons and octopuses have nothing on her.

"Are you subject to nightmares?" asks the well-dressed woman from Albany.

"What the fuck do you think?" replies Nora Swann.

"Night terrors, night sweats, anxiety attacks, insomnia, sleep paralysis?"

"No, no, no. Yes, no."

"Last time, regarding night sweats, you replied in the affirmative," says the well-dressed woman. "Deviation noted."

Nora Swann rubs her eyes, then looks at the images on the wall again. You'd imagine the spooks back in New York could spring for an actual screen, she thinks, but doesn't say it out loud. On the wall, she's carrying a shopping basket holding three containers of gooseberries and a plastic bag of lemons. She'd already explained to one vendor that she was making preserves, following her grandmother's recipe. That morning, her Drogheda brogue had been perfection, and never you mind that she was born and raised in Iowa.

"Tell me," says the well-dressed woman, "on the morning of Monday, October 15, what were your mission objectives?"

"The psychiatrist and the albino," says Nora Swann. "Locate and tweep. Keep it simple. Nothing showy."

"I believe you were provided with their names during the briefing," says the well-dressed woman. "Tell me their names, please."

"I wasn't given their names, but you know that. I was only shown photographs. I wasn't given either of their names."

On the whitewashed wall of the rundown cottage, the projector switches to images gleaned from footage confiscated from a third CCTV camera at the market. The video has changed from black and white to color. There are two figures surrounded by a sea of peonies, bundles of flowers displayed in aluminum pails, a rainbow splashed across the market floor.

"Those are the two individuals?" asks the woman from Albany, and she nods at the screen.

"Yeah," says Nora Swann. "That's them. Just like every time before."

"Your attitude is being noted," says the woman. It almost sounds like a warning.

"Blow me," replies Nora Swann. "My shoulder hurts, I'm sick of these bullshit menthol cigarettes, and I need some fucking sleep. Note all that, too, while you're at it."

The woman from Albany doesn't take the bait. She's an iceberg, this one.

On the wall, there's a woman with red hair, frizzy ginger hair tied back from her face. She's wearing glasses. There's a much younger woman with her, holding her right hand. The psychiatrist and the albino. The psychiatrist is wearing a cream-colored cable-knit sweater and jeans. The albino is wearing jeans, a black turtleneck, and a beige raincoat. There's a leather messenger bag on the red-haired woman's right shoulder, and she's holding a bouquet of calla lilies in her free hand. Seeing the two of them again, Nora Swann tenses and her stomach lurches. It doesn't matter how many times she's been made to watch this footage since the American arrived, Nora's reaction is always, invariably the same.

"Are you going to vomit this time?" asks the well-dressed woman.

"I don't think so," Nora Swann tells her, but there's a plastic bucket on the floor, just in case.

"And, forgive me, Nora, but I have to be absolutely sure of this—you're *entirely* certain, these are the two women you were assigned to find on Monday morning?"

"Yes, those are the two women."

"But you don't know their names?"

"No, I wasn't provided that intel. It wasn't in the dossier. It wasn't part of my briefing in Manchester. I have no idea what their names are."

"Tell me your favorite color," says the well-dressed woman.

Nora Swann stares at the wall, at moving pictures painted with light, and then she stares down at her hands. She wonders if maybe she's going to be sick, after all. "Blue," she says. "My favorite color is blue."

"Any particular shade of blue that you prefer?"

Nora Swann nods. "I'm pretty sure it's called Egyptian blue. At home, I have a faience scarab I bought in Cairo. It's the shade of blue I mean."

"And has that been the case as long as you can remember, your affinity for that shade of blue?"

"Sure," says Nora Swann, and then she looks from her hands to the bucket, but the queasiness is beginning to pass. At least that's something. That's more than she got last time through this same interrogation. And the time before that.

The well-dressed woman sits staring at the images on the wall for thirty or thirty-five seconds, and then she asks, "At this point, how far did you judge yourself to be from your targets?"

"Four and a half meters, max," says Nora Swann. "Fifteen feet, give or take."

"And it was your decision to get in that close?"

"It was."

"Your reputation, Nora, is as a sharpshooter. Are you telling me that your briefing did not specify completing your mission from a distance?"

Nora Swann replies, "No, it didn't. That was left entirely to my discretion. The usual arrangement. I was ordered to acquire and neutralize the targets within a designated time frame. How was left up to me." And then, glancing about the cottage, it suddenly occurs to her that she's alone with the well-dressed woman from Albany. She wasn't alone when the projector was switched on, she's sure of that. There was the tech guy, Donncha, and there was the blonde girl named Josie, the girl who's seen to her wounds, who makes tea, who cooks and runs errands. There were four of them, at the start of the session, only four and not five, because Hugh Papadopoulos, her handler for the last three hits, had been asked by the well-dressed woman to please remain outside the cottage until they were finished. The assassin from Iowa has no idea when Donncha and Josie left; she didn't hear them go. She looks back at the images on the wall.

"What year were you first contacted by Albany?" the woman asks her.

"1992, August 1992."

"I didn't ask for the month, just the year."

Standing in that sea of peonies, the albino looks up and directly into the CCTV camera. The girl's eyes are bright blue and her lips are so pale they have almost no color at all. She lets go of the psychiatrist's hand and reaches into a pocket of her raincoat. She takes out a folded bit of paper, also blue—the blue of an Egyptian scarab—and holds it up to the camera, so there can be no mistake about what she's taken from her pocket. It's an origami swan. She smiles, and then she lowers her arm and looks to her left. Which means she was looking at Nora Swann. Ten seconds pass, fifteen, twenty, twenty-three, twenty-three-point-seven, and then, off camera, there's a gunshot, then another, and people begin to shout and scream and run. Neither the albino nor the psychiatrist move a muscle. Both remain perfectly still. In that moment, they could almost be statues, those two.

The image projected on the wall freezes.

Nora Swann lights another of the stinking menthols, the last one in the pack, and she sits smoking and gazing towards the cottage door. She feels a shiver down her spine, the sort of shiver that her mother always said meant a possum had run across your grave, across the place that would one day be your grave. Nora Swann realizes that her hands are trembling. That's new. She wonders if Hugh Papadopoulos is standing on the other side of the cottage door or if maybe he's already on the M7, on his way to Shannon Airport and a flight back to the States.

The well-dressed woman asks, "Do you know, Nora, why you were deemed valuable to the organization, back in 1992?"

"I was never told," answers Nora Swann, and she can hear a tremble in her voice, as well. "I've always assumed it was my service record, my technical proficiency, my kill rate. I've always assumed it was because I'm good at my job."

The well-dressed woman shakes her head, and then she turns around and switches off the projector. At least, thinks Nora Swann, she won't have to watch the rest of it over again, the part where she draws the Glock and puts a round in her own left shoulder and another in her own right foot. She won't have to see herself crumple help-lessly to the floor of the Dublin fruit and vegetable mar-ket. She won't have to watch herself lying there while the psychiatrist and the albino make their getaway.

"No," says the well-dressed woman. "That isn't why. You see, it's easy to find people who are good at your job, who are skilled with guns and knives and who show no remorse about killing. Who are loyal and follow orders to the letter. There is never any shortage of those kinds of people."

"Fine," says Nora Swann. "Then why was I hired?"

"You were hired—that is, we *chose* you—because your psi aptitude and receptivity scores were very close to zero, lower even than average. You were, as regards psionic ability, a null variable. The Hieronymus machine hardly seemed aware you were in the room. More importantly, you demonstrated an almost complete lack of vulnerability to concerted psionic attack, of the sort you suffered in Dublin this past Monday, and that is a rare quality, indeed. So, you were deemed ideal for wetwork involving push operatives and TK hostiles. We see now that assessment was sorely mistaken, even if we don't yet understand entirely how or why the woman in the market was able to do what she did.

"But that's why I'm here, to solve the problem so we don't make the same mistake twice. Now tell me, how old were you the first time you had sex?"

Nora Swann takes a drag on her cigarette, taps ash on the floor, and then she says, "You need to find her sister."

"Her sister? How do you know she has a sister?"

"How I know doesn't matter. You need to find her, as soon as you can. She's much more dangerous, the sister. They're twins. Identical twins."

"Why didn't you mention this before now?" asks the well-dressed woman, and for the first time since her arrival from Albany, she looks as if maybe she's not completely in control of the situation. For the first time, Nora Swann can see a shadow of doubt in her hard eyes and at the corners of her hard mouth.

"I was twelve," says Nora Swann.

"Excuse me?" asks the well-dressed woman.

"The first time I had sex. It was one of my mother's

boyfriends, only I was supposed to call them 'uncles.' I consented. It wasn't rape, except in the legal sense. But you already know all about that. Still, if you'd like to hear it again, if it gets you wet, I'm not going anywhere, am I?"

And then the well-dressed woman from Albany, she gets up and she walks to the other side of the white-washed cottage. She stands near the crucifix, takes out her phone, and makes a call. And Nora Swann sits in the metal folding chair and waits for more questions or a bullet to the brain or whatever it is that happens next.

13.

Late Saturday Night Motel Signal

(ATLANTA/MANHATTAN, 8/9/2035) [PART 2]

I think, here and there in 707, I'll do this one double pay, cadge the network *and* the blippers. Oh, sure, the net will scream, but I do this best of all, they know that, best of anyone, and the swells won't dare kick me.

Now, ful brighter was the shynyng of hir hewe, imo, the Woman in White, Queen Bee, Queen of Diamond-Hard Dicks, Bells, and Whistles. I cannot look away, she's gone so supernova. She stubs out her cigarette in one of those faux rhino-horn ashtrays you find at the duty-free cabooses. This ashtray is a hideous shade of yellow. Details, boys, it's all the devil right in there. Check your style manuals. Check your sixes and check your weapons at the door, natch. I take a long drag on my own smoke and tap ash onto the polished ceramic at my feet.

"*We dislike journalists,*" she says. "*If you'd done your*

homework, you'd know that. We dislike dreamers even more."

When the nuke went off in St. Petersburg, they say that she was there. Sara White Queen, White Queen Black, that is what they say. Though, the two times I *formal* interviewed her not dozing she neither confirmed nor did she deny. She collects sleepy sea shells by the seashore. Did I mention that already? No, yes? Scrollback. But she does. Corks them up, they say, and I dare say she took no few of my own in the twenty-fours we spent one in the other's company. This dream, it's not the day we met. Not at all. I say I spent time in Atlanta, but not with her.

When the tsunami stomped the shivers on Seymour Island, they say she was there, too, swimming with the melting bergs, penguins, and what you'll have.

She's a bad penny, this one.

No one has ever believed I spent waking time in her company. The blippers won't even buy *that* for fact, and they snap up the bat boys and Buddhas in bagels. But. Already in progress, the reverie of a night come and gone, ill met by moonlight. Times down at hoof I could sure have used a cheque, but no one will touch, and that makes me wonder how long her arm actually is, right? If we are all only the saddish puppets she spoke of, for true, and she the puppeteer. I wouldn't put it past, the way no one will finger on my reminiscences of the truth. But here I've done a damn double digression, and neither the suicide nor the dream of Her are on the stage of these words. It's the headache. It usually is, the buggity hurtin' slinging John Henry in my own personal *calaveras de azúcar.* Too many hours logged on the scorch, says the docs the network pays for me to see. Should retire, the docs agree, but not like they're gonna pay the rent, and not as if I have any other marketables. Not about to lay down and take that bodhisattva vow, go Romeo clean. But docs are covering their own wars, sure, and so I don't begrudge.

On the bed, the suicide kisses her blade, puts narrow painted lips to steel. The suits back in the tower are getting annoyed her intestines are still on the proper-born side of her skin. But no one in 707 speaks up to hurry her along, as we all in the know sick to the anticipation. Once it's only the what's done is done, show's over, curtain falls, *die Geschichte ist aus und hier läuft eine Maus,* so drink up, fuckos, until the next kamikaze *puputan* rolls round and you're lucky to be on the guest list.

"*Focus,*" says my bosses.

"*Focus,*" says my memory of WiW.

"*I miss you,*" I say to her, and she laughs.

"*You knew from the start,*" she replies, pull no punch. "*There was never any deceit, unless it was you lying to yourself.*"

She cannot stay in one place that long, for her and thee to last out. Then again, the rumors say she don't gotta, the rumors what say she has a twin white shadow. Ivoire and Bête, but I never asked her for the up and up on that word of mouth. Didn't dare, except in the dreams. Only halfsome fool, me. Ask around, you'll hear.

"I know," I say, and she sighs. *"Sorry,"* adds I.

She might two have sighed when the Cat 5 typhoon smucked the fuck down Manila way. She might have sighed, I have thought, all the way before to Hiroshima and Katrina, Peshtigo and Tunguska.

"Why don't you shut up and come to bed," she says (not a qyest).

Isn't that why I've asked her here, and a fraction of my lonely in her absence?

I never recall her getting naked or blow-by-blow from chair to bed, but sure it hardly matters. She's there, bedded, flesh as to marble dusted.

"Yes," I reply. *"I'm coming."*

But I turn back to face the glass and the city all spread banquet below the whichever skyward floor we're briefly inhabiting. There are two bird-shaped smears printed on the glass, blood and shit and feathers. Crash, delete. She says I shouldn't look at those, and I know how right she is. But I worry them, regardless, knowing of a certain they are critical integers of the riddle of She.

Nonetheless, don't know, paper toe.

She is a surprisingly gentle lover. In dream, I mean, but, then she was, too, for reals.

Blister white here, though in 707 a bead of the αἷμα swells holly-berry gleam on our suicide-to-be's mouth after a first unexpected slice, not qyest inadvert. She licks it away, but has earned from the pit a grateful ah-now-all-sit-up-take-notice sigh. Set aside your idle conversation. Her second, she'll have to take up sword should prime *de dibujo* etc., turn McNuggets on the talismonger assembled, so obviously a second has interest vested in keeping the show must go on. She leans to an ear and whispers. Can't hear, but I can imagine, can't I? Could be, *Make it quick.* Contrawise, could be, *With mercy for the greedy, dear, for rats live on no evil star.* I likes, tho, *Don't you fucking make me do it for you.*

"Carlisle, can you please get a close up?" asks impatient'd, long-suffering producer. I feel the techs scrambling behind my retina. I tab their close-up, sticking to roughshod p's and q's and dot my eyes.

"You got it, you jackal shits," says I. I blink and pull in. It's a good smart shot, if I do concede, and it'll be turning up in the verts and broadsides for months. So close are the second and her Duke of Welly, they might be exchanging sweet nothings. That'll get the viewers at home

and in the *izakaya* and sports bars and bear gardens with wet panties, all right.

All right.

I think the woman with the jellybean hair might be crying, for no added charge.

"You getting all this, Carlisle?"

I am.

In my Deep South Peachtree dream, the Queen Bee holds me. She smells of tobacco, vanilla, sweat, and semen. We are spent, the both. She does not love me, as there is just one love in her, and she dare not speak its name, so all I have is second-guess work. But the fucks were all good, alike to the dream.

Now trewly, how sore that me smarte ashen dede and colde.

I would live down the *vieux rêve* forever. I'm that pathetic.

And finally like 707 She Here To See does as promised the johnny comes, and before she loses her nerve straight in dives the *tantō*! Huzzah and hallelujah!

The sponsors will be not complaining, no, and the net will be happy-happy, and here's your pound of flesh, you at home (or wheresomever). And, important most the all, I get paid my commish. Huzzah! Homerun! Into the belly, then cutting traditional left to right, ah, you see? I always am put to mind by the entrails of pink-blue deep-sea worms, fat on rotten abyssal carrion. Ever see a clip of hagfish at a down-below whale fall? Still-living intestines in my view, they seem to writhe like that. The room gasps a collective gasp, as traditional as the dictates of this perverted seppuku. I'm right there, covering the war, and in the hollow dogging the shoes of that gasp is when I spot her, Her, Woman in White and Of White and Queen-Be Ivory Beast. Sara Never Was Her Name, but one amongst a hundred. Here's rumor made manifest, my Johnny comes.

"*Woolgathering?*" in ATL asks me.

At the Chinatown present-day, I have dared divert my attention from the bed, in danger of scotching the *grande* eloquent *hacer un exit,* which could or shall cost me of a certain a percentage. But I feel as of old her eyes on me, in that aftergasp, which is how not could I fucking look? Right? Yes, no? Yes, kanga and yes, more roo. This will pass so fastly, as did that sword through the woman's innards, as always passes climax, orgasm, all fine pinnacle gained. This will pass like a bolt from the blue. We'll not speak. I would not hazard to go half that distance. Chillsome bumples on my arms and legs and hairs up on the back of my neck, since—rumors and my true intent aside—what the motherfucking Christ is she doing here? Has she come for me or only for the gladiatorial entertainments? Has she come back to stay? It's a domino toppling towards the next in line, no doubt, and this is why, sure, there's more fear in me than deelite at the sight of her.

"*Just thinking,*" I reply.

"*Only just thinking?*"

"*The crows,*" I say, then roll off her and nod towards the window and the bird-shaped stains. "*Are they here for you? Or only because of you?*"

For, even asleep, I do not believe in coincidentals.

"*You should rest,*" she shushes.

The woman on the bed in 707 slumps forward, though not yet dead, still short of bag and tag, and the crowd goes wild. Her second kisses her cheek. See thee off to an honorable end, for they speak of honor in the fulfillment of one's Art, and if this is not art I don't know what would be. Crimson pigment splashed upon the canvas of the real.

I am able not to hear the angry from the tower, good at my bithead's lookaway when I gotta be, when I've blown code but good and the coyote's get forlorn, for live paid extra for an under the counter, backroom, and costing didn't approve it cut-out chip.

From my dream, says the WiW, Sara White Queen, "*Oh, why so green and lonely? Little lamb, smile.*" Which she does for me, not answering on the issue of corvid sacrificials.

But waking, this night, 707, she does not even approach me. And I respect that, however might it make my soul crumple. We've an agreement. *"Carlisle, you stupid son of a bitch. The bed. Look at the goddamn bed."*

Yeah, this night's gonna have twice-over paydata fat cat credulous scores, and also is it now occurring to me what the alleys will pony for a glimpse who might be her. Oh, it'll rake some nuyen I can stash for drizzle days. But I cover the war, my cover story, and so I do return my focus to death unfolding on the bed.

In the dream, crows hover, and . . .

"What'll I do, when you are far away, and I am blue, what'll I do?"

She shushes me. "Here is the day," says she.

Good nite.

14.

折り紙設計/*Hasenohr Faltung*

From the passenger-side seat of the rented Nissan, Bête stares up at the cold Irish sky, at the low, moldy scum of clouds pressing down on the world, and she says to Doc Twisby, she says, "A slow sort of country. Now, *here,* you see, it takes all the running *you* can do to keep in the same place. If you want to get somewhere, you must run at least twice as fast as that." And Doc Twisby asks her why she's quoting the Red Queen, and the albino twin fingers the shiny black ammonite she wears on a chain about her throat and says, "That tree back there," not bothering to explain which tree, "we've passed it several times already." Doc Twisby in the driver's seat, she assures Bête that it almost certainly isn't the same tree—after all, they've likely passed hundreds of trees since they got on the great asphalt crescent of the M50 at Palmerstown, headed north and then east, headed for the docks and a ferry out of Ireland. Repeatedly, she's told the twin how they got lucky at the fruit and vegetable market the day before, but luck being what it is, they shouldn't expect to get lucky again. Bête is folding thin sheets of crimson and green and lavender *washi* from an origami shop on Camden Street, folding paper cranes. Since she began just after dinner the night before, she's folded a whole boxful, but one can never be too cautious. "Step three," she says aloud, "fold the triangle in half by taking the left corner and folding it to the right. Step four, take the top flap and open it, then crease both the right and left sides so that you can fold the top corner to the bottom corner." Twisby, she says, "Dear, you probably have enough by now," but Bête shakes her head, and Twisby, she doesn't argue. She's learned to trust the twin's intuition in these, and most other, matters. They pass blue exit signs printed in English and in Irish, and they pass other drivers and freight trucks and delivery vans, and Doc Twisby assures Bête that the turnoff for the ferry isn't much farther, and Bête, she assures the doc that they've just passed that same tree again. "You're sure?" asks Doc Twisby, and the twin, she speaks in the raspy voice she always uses when she's quoting the Red Queen, "That's right, though, when you say 'garden'—*I've* seen gardens, compared with which this would be a wilderness." Doc Twisby nods and keeps her eyes on the road. When they reach France, she can try to sort out whatever it is that's happening to the twin's psyche, whatever began when Bête folded an assassin that Albany had sent to murder them both—dissociative fugue, depersonalization, transient schizoaffective disorder, what the fuck ever it is that's been shaken loose or turned wrong way around inside her head. These things are to be expected. These things were always inevitable. She is treading ground never trod before. "We're being watched, you know," says the twin, "we're being followed." And Twisby says, "Yes, love, but not by a tree, we're not." And Bête tells her, "She'll kill us, if she ever finds us." Doc Twisby asks, "Who? Who will kill us?" Bête, she says, "Step fourteen, take the right flap and fold it over to the left—in this instance, the left being north. Take the right flap and fold it north. I mean the Egyptian, *le Juif errant, Jerusalemin suutari.*" They're coming up on the entrance to the Dublin Tunnel, and traffic has slowed to a crawl. "She's not going to find us," says Doc Twisby, and the twin counters, "And Jesus said, 'I shall stand and rest, but thou shalt go on till the last day.'" Doc Twisby scowls and says, "Don't make her into more than she is. She's only a woman, no matter how much nonsense and mystique and no matter how many tall tales Barbican wraps round her." The twin folds her crane, and she glances at the windshield, and she glances up at the low, moldy sky above the windshield, and in her Red Queen voice she says, "You *say* that, love, but we run like rabbits, and you may call it 'nonsense' if you like, but *I've* heard nonsense, compared with which that would be as sensible as a dictionary. Call it nonsense, and I will call us rabbits, and all the world will be your enemy, Prince with a Thousand Enemies, and whenever they catch you, they will kill you." *But first they must catch you,* thinks Doc Twisby, and she checks the clock on the dashboard and worries about missing their boat. "I'm not even certain that she's Egyptian," says Bête, speaking in her own voice, beast twin, white shadow, pale fugitive. "Though she's thought of herself as Egyptian so long now that I doubt she remembers the truth of it. She may be Persian. She may be Ethiopian. She may be the Queen of Sheba herself." Bête pauses, then adds, *"Nigra sum, sed formosa,"* and crosses herself, and then she recites steps nineteen through twenty-one. "Now," she says, "step twenty-two: bend the wings downward at a ninety-degree angle, and you've finished a splendid origami crane." Doc Twisby, she asks how many that makes now, and the twin looks at the old shoebox of paper cranes in the back seat and replies, two hundred and ten. "So, just a few more then?" asks the doc, and the twin nods her head, yes, just a few more. The traffic is moving again, and before long the tunnel swallows them down its long concrete gullet, and now there's no looming, conspiratorial sky to bear witness against them. No grey October sky to press them beneath its thumb. And no lurking, recurring trees. Bête wishes they could stop here. She wishes they could be like proper rabbits, like any good child of El-ahrairah and hunker down in the darkness broken only by the glaring LCD lights mounted on the tunnel ceiling, that they could dig in and wait until the wolves and the stoats and the hungry hunting birds with hooked claws and hooked beaks have all gone away. They could wait here, she thinks, until the Egyptian loses interest, until the storm blows over and her dying, divided sister finishes fighting monsters in Maine, until poor, brave Ivoire isn't dying anymore, until Ivoire crosses the sea on triumphant white wings and finds them waiting in the gloom. Bête presses her face to the window and watches the whitewashed cement walls rushing past. "Quietness is wholeness at the center of stillness," she says. "The only evil is waste." These words rattle off her tongue like rosary beads pinched between pious Catholic fingers. She shuts her eyes for a moment, only to find Nora Swann waiting there for her. The assassin dutifully shoots herself, and Bête opens her eyes again and stares at the white tunnel wall. "You'll like the ferry, I think," Doc Twisby tells her. "Will I?" asks the Red Queen, speaking from the lips of the twin. "Look up, speak nicely, and don't twiddle your fingers all the time. Why will I like the boat?" And so Doc

Twisby tells her, "It's called the MS *Oscar Wilde,* and it will carry us to Cherbourg. It has a movie theater and restaurants and a perfume shop. It even has a beauty salon." *Everything I'm saying is beginning to sound absurd,* Doc Twisby thinks to herself. *Lewis Carroll would be amused.* Situation and anxiety is rendering her every word in shades of nonsense. "It has a maximum capacity of 1,458 passengers," says Bête. "Any one of them might be an operative, a butcher for Albany or a butcher for Y or even one of your own who has decided they don't like the way you're playing the game." Doc Twisby gives her a look, gives the twin such a look it would do murder if looks worked that way, and then the psychiatrist, she says, "That, my dear, is why you're folding cranes. Now, you should stop staring out the window and get back to it." She doesn't ask the girl how it is she knows how many passengers the ferry can hold. She's learned enough to know there's no use in asking questions. But Bête, she's thinking how maybe this tunnel runs on and on forever, and how, if maybe it does, they won't ever need all those cranes, after all. How maybe they can just keep going until the Nissan finally runs out of gas, and then what? *The horse is dead. From here we walk,* she thinks. And then she says it aloud. "What?" asks Doc Twisby, and in the tale unfolding behind the twin's eyes, the Red Queen says (and so says Bête), "I wonder if I shall fall right through the earth. How funny it'll seem to come out among the people that walk with their heads downwards! The Antipathies, I think." Doc Twisby, sitting there behind the wheel, one wary eye on the road ahead and one warier eye on the twin, she answers, "I think perhaps you've got the story mixed up again, love. Mind your page numbers. Mind the volumes." But Bête, she says, "I wonder what Latitude or Longitude I've got to?" as if the psychiatrist hasn't spoken a word. And then she turns her face away from the window, away from the tunnel wall rushing past outside, and Twisby feels herself being peered into, and she knows this is what it felt like to be Nora Swann. And she thinks what Victor Frankenstein must have thought, staring into the eyes of his creature, and she expects the girl to open her mouth and say (for example), "I ought to be thy Adam, but I am rather the fallen angel." Instead, Bête says, "We don't have to take the ferry. We don't have to swim the ocean. We don't have to fight the tide. We could stop right here, like all the people of El-ahrairah, and we could wait for Ivy to find us. We could be cunning and dig deep. Who'd think to look for us here?" And in this moment, and not for the first time, Doc Twisby, she sees her possible doom and the possible doom of many other things besides crouched here behind the impenetrable blue eyes of the twin. *Victor Frankenstein,* she thinks. *Yes, but also Oppenheimer and also Marie Curie and Einstein and a thousand other well-meaning fools who reached for the stars and lived to wish they'd not been half so ambitious, half so curious, half so clever and willing to trespass on the domain of a thousand different deities, who were always fools themselves.* "You flatter yourself," Bête tells her, and the psychiatrist can almost feel the way the twin is rummaging around inside her head, squeezing in between left and right hemispheres, insinuating herself into cortical folds, between the grey matter topography of gyri and sulci. In the gloom beneath the earth, Doc Twisby sees or only imagines that she sees the predatory glint of red-gold eyeshine boring into her brain and into her soul, but there's no mistaking the twin's sudden mood swing, and there's no mistaking the desire to do harm crouched between the angry words of her experiment. Bête says, "What we have done to Ivy, we *deserve* to die for that, you and I *both*. But you most of all. You deserve to die a thousand times over, for what you've done to her, for sending her away to fight a Jabberwocky with only that lunatic Sixty-Six at her side. Never mind the disease and the dope, you have not even warned her, have you? But I could stop it now. You don't *think* that I know that, but I do. I could stop it *all*, right this very second, couldn't I?" And Doc Twisby, not quite managing to hide the tremble in her voice, she says, "We're almost out of the tunnel, love. We're almost to the boat.

And remember, quietness is wholeness at the center of stillness, and the only sin in all the world is waste. We stop now, and it's all been a waste, it's all been for nothing, all of Ivoire's pain and all your fear and sorrow and all of our running." But turbulent, seditious Bête, she says how maybe she doesn't care anymore. How maybe she's perfectly happy being a sinner in the hands of an angry god, if that means she can only put her arms about her sister again, and if that means she never has to have a gun aimed at her head again, and if it means, also, that she never again has to force an assassin to turn that gun on herself. "Don't you think I *know* we're all but off the reservation now?" asks Bête of Doc Twisby. "Don't you think I *know* you're flying blind, pretty much making it up as you go along, because maybe you're afraid Julia Set's about to cut her losses and pull the plug on your little horror show? Maybe it wasn't Albany that sent Nora Swann. Maybe it was the dogs who hold *your* chain." Now there's a bright pinpoint of pain behind Doc Twisby's eyes, and she knows that in another few seconds, or less, the twin could *fold,* just the same as she's been folding all those many pretty *orizuru* against their ruin. For Bête, it would be almost the easiest thing in the world. So, with nothing left to lose, Doc Twisby screws up a mad scientist's bottomless gall and audacity, and she quotes from a book she's read the twin twice over now, a book she's sewn through and through with suggestion and post-hypnotic contingency: "Tearing the paper means you've stopped believing in the infinite possibilities of a square," she says, hardly louder than a whisper. And—just for a few seconds more—Bête glares defiantly back at her like a caged and tortured tiger, like a wild and hurting thing ready to break free and be done with its captivity—but *then,* then the rebellion is quashed and all the fight drains out of her and here again is only half a will, only a half portion of resolve, only sweet, compliant Bête who wants nothing but to get all those paper cranes folded, just in case another wolf comes knock, knock, knocking at the door. And the car exits the tunnel into dim, clouded day that seems, by comparison, almost bright as the surface of the sun, and Doc Twisby is ashamed at her relief and ashamed, too, at the way her hands are shaking when she pays her €3 at the tollbooth. She passes the receipt to Bête, and the twin makes of it another crane. "You'll like the ferry," says Doc Twisby to her little white lab rat. "You'll like Paris. I'll take you to the natural history museum on the rue Cuvier, and you can see the dinosaurs there. You can tell me all about them." And Bête, she asks, "Do you think that would be safe? Don't you think that's just the sort of place they'll be looking for us?" And Doc Twisby pretends to smile a wise and knowing smile, and she tells the twin, "We shall see, little beastie. We shall see."

15.

The Spider's Stratagem

(LONDON, 12/12/2012)

Ptolema taps ash, ash from her first cigarette in fifteen years, onto the polished floor of the Commissioner's study. The tiles are cut from beds of lithographic limestone mined near Langenaltheim, Germany, the same quarry where the first specimen of *Archaeopteryx* was discovered in 1861. If the Commissioner objects to cigarette ash on his Jurassic floor, he's kept it to himself. Maybe he's too absorbed in their game of chess to notice, or it may simply be that he doesn't care. Ptolema takes a long drag, exhales, and considers her next move. The Commissioner takes chess very seriously, and it wouldn't do to let on that she truly has no interest in whether she wins or loses. It wouldn't do to put the man in a disagreeable mood this evening, not with her report still freshly landed on his desk.

Ptolema sees that she can win in eleven moves and

tries to decide whether or not to throw the game, whether or not it's necessary, and if he'd know. He is a strange man, even among this bevy of strange men and women, and she has long since learned that second-guessing the Commissioner is a perilous undertaking, indeed.

"That disagreeable woman in Dublin . . ." he begins and trails off, lifts his black knight, then returns it to the board. "I do trust that you were quite thorough before taking care of her?"

"I'm certain of that, sir."

"Ptolema, my dear, no one is ever fucking certain of anything. In all the wide world, there is not a scintilla of certainty."

Ptolema keeps her eyes on the board.

"After that business by the river, I tracked her down and put two bullets in the back of her head, and another in her chest. I weighted the body and sunk it in the river. Unless the Xers have mastered necromancy, you may rest assured she's out of the picture."

"I never rest assured of anything." He sighs, lifts the knight a second time, and, a second time, returns it to the board.

"She's dead, sir."

"And that other one?"

"Her, too. Three bullets, same as the redhead. With all

due respect, meting out death is one of the few things at which I excel. I've been doing it . . . seems like almost forever."

"It wasn't an insult, Ptolema. You ought to know enough to know that. But I like to hear these things delivered directly from the horse's mouth, as it were. Paperwork is all well and good, but it cannot replace my ability to glean the truth of a situation from the timbre, the tonality, of a human voice."

She has heard it said that the old man is a living, breathing polygraph machine. She's heard it said he's as good as a syringe of sodium pentothal or thirty seconds of waterboarding. Only an idiot would lie to the Commissioner, but, even within the ranks of their organization there are very many idiots, though their tenure inevitably proves short.

"Understood, sir."

"Is it a fact that you once played Wilhelm Steinitz?" he asks her, studying the board, clearly aware of her advantage. "I have heard that, but one hears so many fairy tales."

"I did," she replies. "In 1892, before he lost his title to Lasker."

"And you beat him?"

"No, sir. Stalemate, after fifty-two moves. Queen versus pawn, but his pawn had advanced to its seventh rank."

"Still," he said, "Steinitz. What I would have given just to have seen that game. Now, how about the Twisby woman?"

"It's in the report—"

"Bugger the ruddy report. I asked *you*, did I not? Where do we stand in regard to that slippery bitch?"

"No one's seen her since the seventh of November, when she was spotted in Paris."

He swears and dithers over his one remaining knight.

"You knew that already," she says, and he looks away from the board only as long as it takes him to scowl at her. "But, at this stage, she hardly matters," the Egyptian continues. "Not with a double agent in place on-site. We give the kill order, and it's over. To be frank, I don't understand why it wasn't given a month ago. The longer we wait . . ."

He shakes his head and leans back in his chair, as if ready to surrender the game.

"Complications," he sighs. "Protocol."

"Since when do we acknowledge even the *existence* of protocol among terrorists?"

"Since, my dear, no one wants to see these parlor games escalate into all-out war. *That's* since when."

Ptolema nods and sends a series of smoke rings towards the ceiling. The third time Ptolema met with the redhead, fifteen minutes before her execution, she'd said,

"What Twisby told me, and I quote—more or less, so maybe I should say 'paraphrase,' instead—'What if Einstein had needed a small push to get him moving? What if, say, Oppenheimer or Fermi had needed a bit more motivation? That's all this is. Bête and I providing her sister a bit more motivation, so her skills are not wasted among petrified bones and dusty museum drawers. That's all.'"

The Commissioner says, "Also, it would be preferable, would it not, if our cryptographers made sense of that message before we dispatched the twin?"

"Right," Ptolema says, hardly bothering to hide her sarcasm. "The twin."

"Clearly this Thisby person has washed her hands of the girl, the way she's on the move."

"Twisby, sir. And that may be true. Or it may be true that she's accomplished her mission, and there's nothing left to do but wait."

The Commissioner mutters, then picks up his knight, and quickly, before he can change his mind, moves it to the king's second square. Ptolema immediately takes it with her one surviving white knight. She has him in four more moves.

She's thought before, and here she thinks again, how much the Commissioner looks like John Tenniel's interpretation of the White Knight from *Through the Looking*

Glass. The same absurd mustache. The same beak of a nose. All he needs is a sway-backed horse and spiked anklets to guard against shark bites. The White Knight sang, *"I look for butterflies, that sleep among the wheat . . ."*

Only, the Commissioner always plays black. Or maybe only when he pits himself against her.

"Blast," he mutters and pours himself another brandy from the decanter on the table. "Blast your arse. You might at least have pretended to be taken off your guard."

"Apologies, sir. Your move."

He takes a sip of the brandy. "In your expert estimation, Ptolema, am I both imbecilic *and* blind? I can *see* the bloody board."

"Neither," she replies. "A question, though. Have you considered that there's no code to crack?"

He looks at her as if she's the imbecile.

"I mean," Ptolema continues, "hasn't anyone considered the . . . outside chance . . . that the message is meant to be taken *literally?*"

His expression doesn't change, and he doesn't answer her. For a few seconds, the study is so quiet she could hear a mouse fart, were one to choose just then to do so.

"More a sort of roundabout, cockeyed sort of exposition, sir. 'Black queen white, white queen black.' And then the second part, the Trenton transmission, 'To see themselves, they're gazing back.'"

"I *know* the blasted rhyme, Ptolema."

"Of course. But it seems to me everyone's been so busy assuming it's the usual cryptic shit we get from the Xers, no one's even paused to—"

"This is in your report?" he asks. He drains his glass and watches her.

"No," she says. "It isn't."

"Odd, given it appears to have aroused in you some considerable passion."

"It only occurred to me just this morning. I was standing in front of my bathroom mirror, brushing my teeth, and—really, it was the mirror that set me thinking there might—"

"You have me in four," he says. "And I despise futility."

"Do you want to hear this, sir? Because, if you don't, I'll shut the fuck up. I know I'm out of line. I don't have to be told this isn't my department."

"I would have thought, my dear, that in all those centuries you've seen come and go, you'd have learned to stand your ground. I have until a quarter of," and he points at the immense grandfather clock occupying one corner of the study.

The Commissioner pours himself another drink. And Ptolema tells him what's on her mind, a hunch that might be nothing more than that, but a hunch that succeeds in explaining almost, but not quite, everything they know.

While she speaks, she contemplates the cross-section of a fossil ammonite preserved in the polished limestone floor. The logarithmic spiral echoes across the universe: the arms of the Milky Way; a moth to a flame; the configuration of corneal nerves; the bands of a typhoon; a fractal seahorse tail of a Misiurewicz point.

Ptolema talks.

The clock rings the hour, and he doesn't interrupt her. As she goes on, his expression changes from skepticism to disbelief to the very last thing she ever expected to see him show, something she'd wager her left hand is fear.

16.

Now[here] Man Saves/Damns the World

(ALBANY, 12/20/12)

In the labyrinth of fluorescent lights and numbered doors beneath the subbasment of the Erastus Corning Tower, the Signalman sits behind his desk and thinks the unthinkable. When you come right down to it, that might as well be the first and only line in his job description, if men like him ever were given the simple courtesy of job descriptions. The stark black hands of the round white clock hanging on his office wall, right next to a portrait of the president, say it's twenty-five minutes until midnight. Tick-tock, tick-tock, and now it's even less than that. He takes out the antique pocket watch that goes with him everywhere, the antique silver railroad watch that once was his great-grandfather's, and he checks the clock on the wall against it. The two are in all but perfect accord, give or take a handful of seconds, and what the hell difference is that going to make, when all is said and done. He closes the silver watch and lays it on his desk next to the MacBook Pro sitting open in front of him. The Signalman glances up at the water stain directly above his desk, like a bruise or a carcinoma marring the interlocking tiles of the dropped ceiling, and he thinks about the great, wide world above. Tonight, he can feel all the weight of it, crushing and absolute, inarguable as his own mortality, those forty-four stories of steel and glass, concrete and Vermont Pearl marble pressing down like God's own paperweight to hide a billion dirty secrets. To hide him and all his cohorts, Albany's little army of invisible tin men—now you see them, now you don't—soldiers in neat black suits and narrow black ties and black fedoras just like the one Frank Sinatra wore in *Tony Rome*. Somewhere out there, some think-tank asshole probably still believes this makes them inconspicuous.

He spares another glance for the clock on the wall.

Tick-tock, hickory, dickory, dock.

Via the laptop's screen, the Signalman is afforded a perfect satellite's-eye view of the coast of Maine, of Penobscot Bay and the place where Deer Isle ought to be, but isn't anymore. Instead, there's only an oily looking smudge, a roiling, hazy smear to demarcate the brewing of an apocalypse.

The Signalman cracks the seal on a fresh bottle of J&B Rare, and he pours himself two fingers, then says what the fuck and fills the glass almost to the rim. But he has time for just one sip before the door opens, and it's Vance (no knock), and she wants to know if he's made the call, and if he hasn't, what's the holdup? After all, here it is, his hour come around at last, and, by the turn of an unfriendly card, the honor and the horror and all the liability fall to him. His sentence, his encumbrance, his murdered albatross to wear.

"Come on in," he says to Vance, and she hesitates, then steps into his office and pulls the door shut behind her. She looks up at the clock on the wall.

"It's getting late, sir," she says. "You know that, right? They're waiting."

"Don't worry," the Signalman tells her. "The end of the world never starts without us. Read your contract. It's right there in the fine print. You want a drink?" He points at the bottle of J&B, then takes another sip from his glass. "Come on," he says. "Sit down. They're more inclined to call it alcoholism when I drink alone."

Again, Vance hesitates. She's a new hire, siphoned off the FBI's Seattle field office just a couple of years back, and this is the first time she's been around when the balloon has gone up. The poor kid's still getting her sea legs. It's not like she hasn't seen some bad shit. She has, or she wouldn't be here, standing in his office, trying to decide if sitting down for a whiskey with the Signalman is such a good idea right now, all things considered. It's just that there's bad shit and then there's bad shit, and Mary Vance's idea of bad shit is some KKK neo-Nazi skinhead motherfucker from an Idaho militia detonating a dozen barrels of ammonium nitrate, Tovex Blastrite gel, and nitromethane before she catches up with him. Mary Vance's nightmares are populated with domestic terrorists and serial killers, not little green men and extradimensional invaders.

"I insist," he says, motioning to a chair with his glass.

So, Mary Vance sits down, and the Signalman takes another glass from a desk drawer, and he pours her a drink and passes it to her. She stares at the glass, then glances at the clock again.

"Jesus," he sighs, "will you please stop doing that? If you don't, I'm going to get up and pull the damn thing off the wall."

She apologizes and takes a sip of her whiskey, then sits staring at the floor.

"It's not the end of the world," he says, though even he would have to admit there's nothing especially convincing about the *way* he says it. "It's a goddamn mess, sure. It's one for the ledgers. It gets a goddamn gold star by its name, no doubt about it, but it isn't the end of the world. It never is."

Vance doesn't look like she believes him.

"You want to hear a joke?" the Signalman asks her.

"Not especially," she replies. "Not if I have a say in the matter."

"Good and Evil walk into a bar," he says.

"So, I don't have a choice," says Vance.

The Signalman shrugs, and he reaches for the half-empty pack of Camel Wides lying on top of a stack of printouts stamped with catchy, ominous, Secret Squirrel watchwords like *Eyes Only* and *Burn After Reading* and *Cosmic Top Secret*. He takes a matchbook from his shirt pocket, free matches courtesy a dive bar on Jefferson Street called the Palais Royale. A pretty chichi name for a dive bar, but what the hell. He's been going there every night now for the past two weeks, ever since he got yanked from his usual digs in Los Angeles and dropped into the Ant Farm, as the men and women in the black suits have been known to call the offices below the sub-basement of the Erastus Corning Tower. The Signalman lights his cigarette, then drops the spent match into an ashtray that needed to be emptied yesterday. One of the few perks of working this far below the radar is that no one gives a shit if you smoke. No one gives a shit if you drink yourself to death or pop oxycodone or snort enough coke to keep Colombia happy for a year, just as long as it doesn't get in the way of the work. There are no drug tests in Albany and there aren't any no smoking signs, either.

"Of course you have a choice," says the Signalman. "You always have a fucking choice, Vance, and it's no skin off my nose. I was just trying to lighten the mood, that's all. You want the gloom and doom pure and undiluted by levity, have it your own way."

Vance frowns and takes a swallow of her scotch.

"No, it's okay," she says. "Sure, tell me a joke. Good and Evil walk into a bar. What then?"

"No. Screw it. The moment's passed," and he takes a long drag on his cigarette and blows smoke rings at the water-stained tiles overhead, at everything above, at God in his sumptuous gold-plated Heaven, if that's where the fucker really lives. "It wasn't very funny, anyway. You smoke?" he asks and offers her a Camel.

"No, sir. I don't smoke."

"Kids these days," he mutters and steals a peek at the clock.

"It's getting late," she says, her eyes following his. "They're waiting."

He nods, then asks her, "You know what I wanted to be when I grew up?"

"No, sir, I don't."

"Anything but this," he says. "Anything in the whole goddamn universe but this right here. You know what the population of Deer Isle, Maine, was before Sunday, August 12 arrived and turned that place into a Stephen King novel? Just under two thousand human beings, Vance. By now, I figure they're mostly fucking dead. Or worse. But we know some of them are still alive. A hundred, at least. Maybe twice that number. We're still getting a couple of shortwave ham broadcasts coming out of Stonington. The transmissions are staticky and intermittent, but they're there, people asking for help, over and over and over. People wondering if anyone on the outside is still listening. People who, you gotta figure, by now they're starting to think maybe they been marked out as, I don't know, let's say sacrificial lambs, offered up to appease the gods. And after a fashion, they aren't so very far off the mark, are they?"

Vance sets her glass down on the edge of the desk, and then she clears her throat and looks him in the eyes. "Sir," she says, "pardon my asking, but you're not getting cold feet, are you?"

He takes another drag and holds the smoke in until his ears start to buzz. *And what if I am, Vance,* he's thinking. *What if I am. Are you sitting there drinking my whiskey and imagining maybe this is your big break? I lose my nerve, I flinch, I get the heebie-jeebies and you rush in to fill the void? Do you look in my face and see a promotion? Is that how it is, little girl? Is that ambition I smell?* The Signalman thinks about the loaded SIG Sauer P226 in his top desk drawer, and he thinks about the ugly hole it would make.

He exhales, and the silver-grey smoke rolls towards Mary Vance like a fog rolling in off the sea.

"What you just asked me," he says, "I didn't hear that, you understand."

Several long seconds pass before she nods and looks away, before she reaches for the glass of whiskey again, and the Signalman knows that if she didn't need the drink before, she needs it now. He looks at the white clock on the wall, and then he picks up his great-grandfather's silver railroad watch, the watch that earned him his nickname with the agents of Dreamland, with all the spooks and shadow bosses and star chambers from sea to shining sea, and then checks that, too. Both the pocket watch and the clock on the wall agree that there's only seven minutes left until midnight. Zero hundred hours. That magic moment.

Vance finishes her drink in one long swallow. Then she wipes her mouth on the back of her left hand, and she says, "I didn't mean anything by it, sir."

"You didn't mean anything by what?" he asks, and then he closes the MacBook Pro, so he doesn't have to see the live satellite feed off that hazy, ever-expanding smear where Deer Isle used to be. "I have no idea what you mean."

"Yes, sir," she says. "Thank you, sir."

"Don't thank me yet, Vance. Could be this one really is

the end, and I just did you a grave disservice." And maybe she knows what he means, and maybe she doesn't.

"Yes, sir," she says. "Will you be needing anything else?"

"Just some privacy," he tells her. "I have a call to make."

17

Thunder Perfect Mind/Judas as a Moth

(UNDATED)

Estrid Noble sits naked and alone on the wet concrete floor of the small room that, though it *is* a small room, seems to stretch on forever in all directions. Forever and forever and forever. The towering, rumbling Waxen Men have all two gone, but she couldn't say how long since they left her, were she to say anything at all. Which she won't. There is no light in the room save the miserly flicker-glow of a naked twenty-five-watt bulb. One of the Waxen Men bumped his head against the dangling fixture on his way out. He snarled obscenities, not noticing and, surely, not caring how he'd set the light to swinging pell-mell so that it became the arm of a luminous pendulum. It sways from side to side, pushing at the four murky corners of the room that is surely much too small to *have* four murky corners. The shadows are indignant and push right back. The light is a bully. And, if that's so, the darkness is a counter-bully. Or, it is the other way around. Or, such a black-and-white dualism cannot even exist here. But this is where they left her, sick of her again, sick of, they say, her bullshit, and so they left her in this room where the walls seem to stretch on forever. Estrid, her back pressed against freezing, slippery ceramic tiles and mildewed grout. Once upon a time, back before the ghosts of all these imprisoned lunatics, those walls were white as snow, white as the uniforms of the Waxen Men who dragged her howling from Room 66 and left her here. First, they took her clothes and turned the spigots on her, water so cold it would freeze a polar bear in its tracks.

A line, a white line, a long white line . . .

Her honey-colored eyes do the math, calculating angles, the dilapidated geometry of the inside of this cube, the velocity and acceleration vectors of that swinging bulb. Before anyone knew she was insane, she was called a prodigy, carrying the burden of π to 67,393 digits, NaN x 10^{-4} around in her booming, insomniac skull. In this place, hospital, institutional blue, asylum (which does not mean *sanctuary*), neither the doctors nor the nurses nor the Waxen Men will take mercy and give her paper to put the numbers on. She has to keep them all in her head. This she will learn to do forever more.

Four walls that once were white. You can only scrub

so much shit, mold, and, yes, even blood off four walls. Probably, she believes, it has been a thousand years since these walls were genuinely clean. They will never be clean again, for so befouled is their soul, the soul of the walls of this dripping room. A tenth circle of the Inferno. Or an annex to a lesser circle. It is cold as the Arctic here, and she shivers. Hence, it might be the antechamber of the Ninth Circle, possibly the foyer. *Obscure they went through dreary shades, that led along the waste dominions of the dead.*

Xibalba be. A unillumined path through the stars. Six calamitous houses: Dark House, Cold House, Jaguar, Bat, Razor, and Hot House.

She lies down on the floor, anxiety descending, the hollowing-out anxiety of a person who loses a name (for all the Waxen Men will call her is Sixty-Six). Now, right cheek, right shoulder, right side come to rest against the smooth concrete and she stares across that grey manufactured plain towards the faraway door, locked, like Hell, against her escape. Like Hell, no one escapes this place. No one. Five to one, baby. Five to one. She recalls snow and knows all too well that this is the sort of plain that ought to be smothered under a blizzard.

"Tell me, when was the war over?" I asked.

"The war is not over," he answered. "Millions are being killed. Europe is mad. The world is mad."

Not only me. The world is mad, and the we of I, the wee of eye, we will fight in unknown wars.

A line, a white line, a long white line . . .

Through the window of her room, the glass trapped behind a screen of steel diamonds, every winter she watches the snow. It brings more comfort than any of the pills or injections or the sizzling, sparking electrodes to her temples.

This is Hell, and her mother is the Queen of Heaven who damned her.

The Waxen Men are only devils.

The snow is redemption, eternally out of reach.

A line, a white line, a *long* white line . . .

In this room, no snow, just rain to set her to shivering, teeth to clattering, the uncrystallized water from the spigots. Uncrystallizable.

I have mingled my drink with weeping,
And my days are like a shadow.

"You have no one to blame but yourself," said Mother. "You're not sick, you're lazy. You just want the attention. You're not sick, but you can damn well be *treated* as if you are. See how you like that. I've had enough, you hear me?"

So Estrid has her room and the dayroom, never outside, never anything but the glimpse of snow outside, the shower when she's filthy or when the Waxen Men, like Mother, have had too much of her bullshit.

For my days vanish like smoke.

I am like an owl in the desert.

Among the ruins.

A wall, a barrier, toward which we drove.

My God, man. There's bears on it.

Are there? Three bears? A wolf in a red riding hood?

I know numbers, but the walls are high, and I can't climb over.

Estrid Noble lies on the concrete floor, and she lies in snow softly drifting down from a leaden winter sky. Both these things are true, a particle *and* a wave. That, or, instead, the flawed observer, her, the madwoman observer, an emergent, second-order consequence, madness and quantum, madness disbanding paradox. *I don't know what I mean, Mother. I don't know what I mean, anymore.* Has she wrongly believed there is no escape, when, in truth, she can always, always retreat on ragged claws to the snow globe of her unconscious where the Waxen Men cannot follow?

However, lying in the snow, there is blood in the sky mixed with the snow, and she reaches for the shotgun at her side, and she feels the magic welling up within her, which means this cannot be *then*, then consigned to a dustbin of her past, and so this must be *now*.

She sits up in the small room, where the Waxen Men have left her.

She sits up in the snow, where the Waxen Men do not know she can go, which means they cannot stop her and cannot find her when she's here.

She sits up in the small room, realizing someone is watching her from the shadows. Someone indistinct to the left of the door, tucked into that corner, only half revealed when the bulb's glow happens to swing that way.

The someone is another woman, white as a ghost, blue eyes, hair same as the snow.

"I know you," Estrid says, and the pale woman says, "I know you, too."

"How did you find me here?" Estrid asks her.

"It wasn't hard. You split your head wide open. You let me in."

"They don't let anyone in."

"How could they have stopped me?"

Estrid has no answer for that question, but the shotgun feels very good in her hands. At such close range, this is no job for the Kalashnikov, her favorite engine. No. So, her finger's on the trigger of the gasoline-powered, twenty-eight-gauge Remington 1100; this close, she couldn't miss if she tried.

"Sixty-Six," the pale woman says, the albino whose name is Ivoire. Okay, not her name—because the Waxen Men and X stole *all* their names—but the sole name that anyone knows to call her. "Sixty-Six, I would ask you who wants me dead, who's making you do this, but you wouldn't tell me. I know you'd never tell me. You can't, can you?"

"Where are we really?" Estrid asks Ivoire. "Ivoire, *when* are we really?"

"Don't you usually call me Ivy?" the albino asks. "That is, when you bother to call me anything at all. Why are we so formal now?"

The air is bruised with questions.

"Star fall, phone call, no one gets out of here alive," Estrid whispers, hating the way she whimpers like a rabbit in a snare. Isn't she the one holding the shotgun, five to one? Doesn't *she* have the upper hand?

"Your poor spirit," Ivoire sighs. "Shattered, piled up with equations, snippets of song, memories broken apart like twigs. Aren't you tired of being used?"

In an Ithaca asylum, Estrid lies on the concrete shower floor, and in an attic in Maine she holds the barrel of the Remington beneath Ivoire's chin. She blinks, and wishes that just this once, the Waxen Men had forgotten to lock her in with the grout and the dirty wet tiles and the ivory beast. The light swings, and Ivoire's blue eyes twinkle, a flash before the light swings away again, a flash like a falling star plummeting, screaming as it tumbles towards Penobscot Bay.

"I know your secret," she says to Ivoire, and Estrid

smiles a vicious Cheshire cat grin. It's all she has, the se-cret and the shotgun. *If I'd had the shotgun back then, I'd have lain low the Waxen Men. If I'd had the gun then ...*

"But you didn't, Sixty-Six," says the voice from what is momentarily only darkness. "There in the showers, you were naked and helpless. You didn't have anything at all but a dream of snow."

Outside the window of the attic where they sleep, demons are marching out of the sea. Outside the attic window, hardly anyone is left to scream at the sight.

"Tell me the secret," Ivoire urges her, though she doesn't sound the least bit desperate to know. There is no hint of urgency in her voice. "Then we'll both know. If I'm about to die, where's the harm in my knowing?"

"I am now, and I am then," Estrid whispers.

The light shows Ivoire's face, and Estrid thinks she looks a little sad, like whatever's coming is something she doesn't want to arrive.

"A particle and a wave. You are the paradox, Sixty-Six. Free and a prisoner. At now and at then. I know all about that."

Well, I went down in the valley,
You know I did over there ever stay.
You know I stayed right there all day.

"A broken record, that's you," says Ivoire. Estrid tight-ens her grip on the trigger, and she stares up into the bloody snow falling all around her. "And the paradoxical fruitcake, two places and two times at once, if only in your mind."

"Not like you," Estrid says. "Maybe *I'm* a metaphor, but not *you.*"

"Is that your secret, Sixty-Six," and now, ah, now the woman in the corner of the shower room looks nervous. *Dread,* that's the word for her expression. The woman's blue eyes are filled with dread.

"Twin," Estrid growls.

"Yes, Sixty-Six, I am a twin. I have a sister."

In five seconds, Estrid Noble will squeeze the trigger and splatter Ivy's brains across the attic wall. That's already happened.

"No," says Sixty-Six. "Twin. It's not a noun. It's a verb."

She grits her teeth and closes her eyes and fires two rounds. Someone has told her this will save the world. One death. One instant. One action. A butterfly flaps its wings.

18.

Soft Black Stars

Stop me if you've heard this one. Good and Evil walk into a bar . . .

Here: At precisely eight hundred ten hours, the directive came down from on high, effective immediately, cease all evacuation efforts. Additional civilian and military casualties an acceptable loss. Mourn the coming dead *after* zero-zero-thirty of the twenty-first day of December, but blow the goddamn Deer Isle-Sedgwick suspension bridge spanning Eggemoggin Reach, blow it this very night, bury it on the muddy bottom of the leprous bay.

Theirs not to reason why . . .

Finally, all other avenues and efforts and fools' hopes exhausted, they will follow orders, press the red button, implement Operation Umbilicus. Yes, in fact, until this evening the name has seemed hilarious to more than a few. *Who the hell came up with that one, anyway? Don't ask me. I just fucking work here.*

The writing has been on the wall since August, but no one has wanted to read it. No one wanted to believe it would ever go this far, because we are not goddamn Neanderthals huddling in caves by firelight, trembling at the eyeshine Outside, lions and tigers and bears, oh my. Because we are not savages. Because a shoulder to the wheel, and all our technology, and all our beautiful weapons, and all our careful planning, and brave men can solve any situation, no matter how dire. Isn't that motherfucker bin Laden dead? Have we not eradicated smallpox? Are we not making the world safe for democracy? Well, are we not? Do we now leave men and women to die deaths more horrific than any ever imagined by Hollywood, the RAND Corporation, and the Trilateral Commission, science-fiction fucking authors, the alarmists, survivalists, the Book of Revelation, super-secret policy institutes, et cetera and et cetera and et cetera?

"Doesn't seem that way," replies the major general with his two stars on his shoulder. One named Wormwood. The other left unchristened.

A sergeant barks orders, and his men cannot allow themselves to think about the consequences; three have gone rabbit since yesterday, and all three were shot as deserters. Not arrested. Shot. The rest will do their job and see to the

explosive charges, the dynamite, nitroglycerin—the cata-
lysts before the detonation of the linear shaped charges. The
demolition team stands at the ready and have stood so since
dusk. Executioners who are also saviors watch the clocks,
ticking off the bits and pieces of seconds until the implo-
sion of the suspension bridge connecting Little Deer Isle
to the mainland. The bridge uniting Deer and Little Deer
will be left intact. No one knows why. Theirs is most em-
phatically not to wonder why. The deities and demigods in
Washington and the Command Center in Brooksville and
in the Albany Ant Farm have those answers, which has to be
good enough. Good enough for government work. Good
enough to shove a cork in an apocalypse.

לענה

*The third angel blew his trumpet, and a great star fell from
heaven, blazing like a torch, and it fell on a third of the rivers
and on the springs of water. The name of the star is Wormwood. A third of the waters became wormwood, and many
died from the water, because it was made bitter.*

"Buck up, little buckaroo. We're saving the world
tonight."

"Does anyone believe for a minute this is going to
stop . . . that?" And the corporal points at the glistening
sheen smothering the reach, the foulness slick in the sol-
stice moonlight. "Those assholes may as well shoot at an
elephant with a BB gun."

Bows and arrows against the lightning.

The air is being chopped apart with the noise from the rotors of the vigilant Sikorsky UH-60 Black Hawks patrolling overhead. Angles of harsh angels and flat surfaces, terrible swift swords. Do not look at the face of god. Padre, say a prayer for me: *We'd circle and we'd circle and we'd circle, she a laughing giggling whirlybird, my final days in company, the devil now has come for me, and helicopters circling the scene, this is the end, my beautiful friend, this is the end, that's Charlie's point, except you—you were talking about the end of the world, Lord hold our troops in your loving hands, protect them as they protect us, bless them and their selfless acts they perform for us in our time of need, Sed libera nos a malo hosanna, amen, amen.*

"Now, my child, go and sin no more."

Below the bridge, a lumpy round mass more vasty than Leviathan or ten humpback whales is rising from the slime, slime rising from the slime, the star-fall corruption taking shape. It opens one eye.

On the granite boulders north and south of the bridge, the meta-coven of government-requisitioned shamans, witches, and archmages all have begun their chants and sacrifices. Black books have been opened. The first shock wave is their magic . . .

T-minus three minutes and counting.

. . . and the second is the Blacks Hawks' barrage of armaments, laser-guided AGM-114 Hellfire missiles, Hydra 70 rockets, the *chut-chut-chut* bursts from machine and Gatling guns enough to wake the dearly departed. The thing below the bridge bleeds and howls and surges forward. There is no reckoning the anger in that eye. No reckoning whatso-fuckingever. It howls, and now other shapes are rising from the dead waters, answering the call.

"You can't kill the Great Old Ones with shotguns. You may as well grab a goddamn pointy stick."

Write *that* on the shithouse wall.

T-minus one minute.

T-minus forty-five seconds.

Two of the Black Hawks come apart in the air and trail flaming debris across the Maine night sky and raise fire-balls from the haunted forests of Little Deer Isle. Nothing touched the choppers. Nothing at all. They simply came apart.

T-minus . . .

"I'm tellin' you, man. You can't kill fuckin' Cthulhu with a shotgun. Ain't you seen *Godzilla?* Ain't you ever seen *Cloverfield?*"

"Dude, I saw *Aliens,* okay? And guns and nukes worked just fine in *Aliens.*"

"Those ain't nukes, you stupid fuckin' hick. Those *ain't* nukes."

Rotten waves slop against the shore below the bridge, beneath either shore at either end of the bridge—northeast, southwest. The lantern beams of lighthouses carve white clefts across the battlefield, shooing away any who would dare wander near in these last seconds. Lighthouses that still stand and still shine and fuck all knows how that can be. Because the gods have a flair for the cinematic? Deer Isle Lighthouse. Pumpkin Island Lighthouse. Some that ought not to even be visible from this vantage point, but the abominations rising from the reach have begun to warp the fabric of the world, triggering a cascade of gravitational lensing, photons deflected by arcseconds. Mirage.

"Jesus Christ. I can see around corners."

T-minus one second.

Boom.

Men and women turn away. Fall to their knees, are knocked flat on their asses by the blast. Cross themselves. Weep and wail and cover their ears as the bridge announces its deafening death throes and tumbles into the slime, concrete and steel and whipping cables slicing apart monsters, if only for a few heartbeats. If only for the time required for them to coalesce again.

But the bridge is down.

And now it's up to the wards raised by the practitioners of forgotten sorceries, the priestesses who have called out to indifferent heavens, the marshaling of chaotic alchemical elemental Babylonian ninja motherfuckers.

With a little luck and elbow grease, this has only been the *beginning* of the end, the beginning of *an* end.

Punchline: But, then, so is every day. (Rimshot/ Sting) (Cue laugh track)

19.

Where I End and You Begin
(The Sky Is Falling In)

(21/12/12)

"Well, in our country," said Alice, still panting a little, "you'd generally get to somewhere else—if you run very fast for a long time, as we've been doing."

"A slow sort of country!" said the Queen.

"Yes, Sixty-Six, I am a twin. I have a sister."

Alice becomes queen.

Black queen white, white queen black.

Adaptation, counter-adaptation, reciprocation, system instability, runaway escalation.

"Twin. It's not a noun . . ."

This is not the when and certainly not the where that the woman who calls herself Twisby (whose true name—now it can be told—is Lane Dunham, PhD, MD) would have chosen for extraction and reintegration, for the experiment's endgame terminus. Pretty fucking far from optimal conditions. But she's been warned by both Karachi and Kathmandu of two Brit assassins who've been on their asses since the plane touched down at Munich Airport. And, much worse still, the subgnosis pipeline is humming fit to burn with a most ominous forecast: Endgame has been triggered prematurely. The suggestion buried in the subconscious abyss of a hyper-suggestible, third-gen schizophrenic X sleeper agent is surfacing three hours ahead of schedule. Three goddamn hours. So, fuck the architects' precious fucking itinerary; there isn't time to reach the Arstagagan safe house in Uppsala. The architects aren't on the run from bullets. If the trial goes south, they'll just toss the project back to R&D for turnaround at the next best opportunity. Not that a shitstorm like Deer Isle comes along but maybe once a century. Once a century, at best. But, even so, the architects have nothing if not the luxury of time, of second, third, and fourth chances. But Dr. Lane Dunham is only a mortal woman, possessed of ambition and a desire to see the fruits of her labor, and Julia Set was only ever a means to her end. So, fuck X and fuck their contingencies and fuck plan B. She's on her own now, and this abandoned warehouse on the outskirts of Knivsta will have to do. If she tries to make those last sixteen kilometers to Uppsala before retrieving the package, the risk of failure skyrockets to 78 percent.

" . . . it's not a noun."

Her phone rings as she's inserting the IV needle into Bête's forearm, and the twin's trying not to show how scared she is, but the psychiatrist knows her too, too well not to recognize the fear in her eyes.

"Dream," the psychiatrist sweetly murmurs, and the twin immediately falls asleep on the bedroll spread out on the dusty floor surrounded by paper cranes.

Second ring.

Third ring, and she "answers," but you do not say *Hello* when the incoming communiqué has all those zeroes and nothing else *but* zeroes. This call from Julia Set riding piggyback through the mundane transmissions of hacked and repurposed communication satellites, you do not say *Hello*; you hold the phone to your ear and you listen.

Mac OS X speaking for whoever is on the other end of the line, a voice filtered and recorded weeks ago, and here are the words stiffly relayed by Victoria, one-way digital instructions—"And we shall play a game of chess?"

In an attic in Stonington, Maine, a shotgun is pressed to Ivoire's left temple, and the numerical madwoman is about to make love to the trigger.

The psychiatrist drops the phone and it skitters across the floor. Bête's eyelids flutter with the illusion of REM sleep. The portable electroencephalograph converts impulses from the low-density electrode array attached to the twin's scalp, cheeks, and forehead to a tidy display of spike and wave discharges. The IV drips, and the psychiatrist fills a syringe and injects Bête with 0.125 cc's of triazolam. A single, bright crimson bead leaks from her skin. The psychiatrist pops the yellow lid on a mobile automated external defibrillator and powers it up. Just in case. Just in fucking case.

Alice castles. Bête seizes.

"It's not a noun . . ."

" . . . it's a verb."

Black queen white, white queen black.

Six months in the field, and it ends here. Redaction commencing. The EEG beeps, and the sound seems almost deafening inside the empty warehouse. The psychiatrist pulls back the plunger of a second hypo and draws five cc's of diazepam. But precious seconds pass, and the twin doesn't seize after all. By now, Sixty-Six has done her job and done it well, no matter how far ahead of schedule. A soul is careening along the predetermined, nonesuch, ethereal nowhere highway between two continents, simultaneously crossing the Atlantic and an unnamable dreamtime gulf.

" . . . it's a verb."

The psychiatrist leans close and whispers in Bête's left ear, "Checkmate, love. You're home now. Wake up."

" . . . a verb."

And the twin opens her blue eyes.

"You can hear me?" the psychiatrist asks, her voice shuddering with relief. "Bête?"

"Ivoire . . ." the twin croaks, *her* voice raw and groggy.

"Ivoire?" the psychiatrist asks.

"Bête."

The psychiatrist brushes sweaty bangs away from the twin's face. "Now, now, full name, love."

Only a heartbeat's hesitation, and the twin replies. "Lizbeth Elle . . . Lizbeth Elle."

"And surname, please?"

Lizbeth Elle coughs, and the psychiatrist wipes at her forehead again.

"Margeride. Lizbeth Elle Margeride."

The psychiatrist laughs softly, a nervous, relieved laugh. "Good and Evil walk into a bar . . ." she begins.

"But, then, so is every day," answers Lizbeth Elle Margeride. "So is every fucking day." The twin smiles for the psychiatrist; Elle opens her left hand to reveal a vial of liquid from Penobscot Bay, a pearly vial that glows chartreuse, like sickly, trapped fireflies.

20.

ἀποκαλύπτω

(1/5/2013)

Here's the scene: The G-line crosstown local, rattling along the underground throat connecting Queens and Brooklyn. Ptolema sits near the rear of the subway car. She isn't quite alone. There's a black kid at the opposite end, plugged into his iPod and oblivious to all else. There's an elderly Hispanic woman, her purse clutched close to her chest. A man whom Ptolema has taken for either Greek or Turkish sits across from the old woman, reading the *Times.* So, four, only four, and she can live with four. She shuts her laptop and returns it to its carrying case, then stares at the darkness beyond the train's window, which, unfortunately, means staring into her own reflection, which unkindly stares back at her. The negotiations in Albany didn't go well, too many concessions when she can't understand why they've made any at all. Moreover, the cover story that would attribute the Deer Isle Incident to a reactor meltdown aboard a *Seawolf*-class nuclear submarine, to the ensuing explosion and quarantine, is just short of absurd. Perhaps the wipes were potent enough that no one much, military or civilian, quite remembers the events of the twenty-first of December, no one who's not meant to remember. But she seriously doubts the Navy patrol, the US Army, and one collapsed bridge is going to keep that secret a secret forever. Fortunately, everyone was too busy freaking out over Maine to even broach the subject of Twisby's twinning experiment. There isn't the least sense of vindication knowing that the theory Ptolema passed along to the Commissioner more than three weeks ago, the theory he then handed up to the Council, appears to have been correct. Lucky fucking guess. Intuition come too late to intervene.

Reflected in the safety glass, her eyes look every bit as ancient as they are, every bit as weathered as her spirit. At the meeting, no one dared use her name. Only the Egyptian, two words to signify and summarize all the ages of an inexplicably long life. She lowers her head, hiding from the window, too much there to despise. Maybe she'll shut her eyes and try to sleep. Maybe she'll be lucky, and there will be no dreams.

Maybe pigs will fly.

"Stop me if you've heard this one," says the albino woman standing in the aisle, the woman who definitely *wasn't* there only a minute and a half before. She's wearing a cream-colored Gore-Tex parka, ragged jeans, black wraparound sunglasses. Cheap sunglasses. There's a polished, cross-sectioned ammonite on a silver chain around her neck. She glances towards the other three passengers, nods, then turns back to Ptolema. The albino, the twin who is not now and never was a twin, the cipher, the Black Queen who is the White Queen, and vice versa.

To see themselves, they're gazing back.

"See," she says, taking the seat on Ptolema's right, "In the beginning, God created the heavens and the earth. But, right off, he was hit with a class-action suit for failure to file an environmental impact statement."

"I've heard it," Ptolema tells her. "Probably before you were born."

The albino pretends to look disappointed.

"Bête," Ptolema says, whispering as softly as a falling leaf. "Ivoire. Lizbeth Elle. The Ivory Beast. What am I supposed to call you?"

"Elle's fine, but you can speak up," the albino says and motions to the other passengers. "It's not like they can hear us. Hell, they can't even see me, unless the mojo coming out of Harlem these days isn't what it used to be."

"Do I talk, Elle?" asks Ptolema. "Or do I listen?"

"Some of both, though that wasn't my decision. Anyway, we don't have too long before the next station, so, you know. Choose your words wisely."

"Still a lot of unanswered questions, Elle. A lot of people in your own organization pissed off for being left out of the loop regarding Dr. Dunham's enterprise."

"Too bad there isn't ever going to be time for all those answers."

"You're not sick."

"Nope," Elle replies and smiles. "Crazy lady with a shotgun back in Stonington, she was good enough to dispatch that malignancy."

"I don't get the elaborate cloak-and-dagger, dog-and-pony show," Ptolema says, watching both their reflections now. "The bread crumbs. The informants. The meetings in Dublin. The pirate broadcasts and the graffiti. No one ever had to know shit about what you fuckers were up to."

"You'd have to ask Twisby about that," sighs Elle. "I didn't even know myself. That is, during the procedure, so far as I knew, every bit of it was gospel. We were two. The we of I and all that. Quietness is wholeness at the center of stillness, et cetera, blah, blah, blah."

"Both personae were real? Both were corporeal?"

"Abracadabra."

"The particle and the wave."

"Exactly. But we're almost out of time, like I said. And

I suspect your people are already busy running every imaginable computer simulation to determine every imaginable outcome to all these ripples. That is, if they're not too busy with the shoggoths."

"The what?"

"Sorry. The girl who killed me, that's what she called that nasty crap kept crawling out of the bay. Shoggoths."

"You and Deer Isle," Ptolema says. "We don't think that was a coincidence. We don't think it was only a happy, convenient accident. We think—"

"—a lot of crazy shit, and only time will tell. Maybe Twisby built herself the Second Coming of Jesus Christ. Or, it may be I'm the *Anti*-Christ. Shiva. Maitreya. Take your pick. Or maybe I'm only a trial run, a dress rehearsal for the *Big* Show, so nobody of consequence. Nothing at all but a nerdy girl who wants to go back to her stones and bones."

"That would be a waste," Ptolema says.

What if Einstein had needed a small push to get him moving? What if, say, Oppenheimer or Fermi had needed a bit more motivation?

Waste is the only evil.

"Okay," Elle says. "My turn." She digs a thumb and index finger into a pocket of her jeans and pulls out a single .45-caliber cartridge. It gleams dully beneath the subway car's fluorescent lights. "This was meant for you."

Ptolema gazes down at the bullet.

"Then why am I still alive?"

"Ripples," says Elle Margeride. "I think it's about time I began making a few of my own. Here is the day, hmm? Twisby's a sweetheart, and she means well, but she's also the one went and made a queen out of a pawn. She needs to start taking that into account."

And then Elle slips the cartridge into Ptolema's hand and stands up.

"Is this the last time we'll meet?" Ptolema asks, trying not to think about how heavy the bullet feels.

Elle shrugs. "We'll know if it happens, maybe about a trillion dominoes from now."

Ptolema tastes metal, and she licks her dry lips. "There are people looking for you and Dr. Dunham. You know that, right? They catch up with you, they won't be merciful. You've made an impression."

"Introduced a new variable," says Elle, and she pokes a finger at the bridge of her cheap sunglasses.

"One last question?"

"Okay. One last question."

Ptolema sits up straighter, glancing at the bullet and then back to the albino.

"Do you miss her? Your sister, your lover. If both of you *were* real—"

But then Lizbeth Elle Margeride is gone, as unceremoniously as she appeared, and, once again, there are but four other people in the car. Ptolema shuts her eyes and leans her head back and tries to concentrate on nothing but the rhythmic throb of steel wheels on the rails.

APPENDIX 9.

[le remix Anglaise]
Bury Magnets. Swallow the Rapture.

(17 VRISHIKA, 2152)

She sits on a bench in the main observation tier of the *Nautilus-IV,* her eyes on the wide bay window set into the belly of the station, the icy spiral of the Martian northern pole filling her view. *She* being the White Woman. *La femme albinos. Ca-ng bái de. Blancanieves.* More appellations hung on her than all the words for god, some say. But if she has a true name—and doesn't everyone?—it is her secret and hers alone. A scrap of knowledge forever lost to humanity. So, her blue eyes are fixed on the Planum Boreum four hundred kilometers below, yes, but her mind is on the Egyptian—Ancient of Days, el Judío Errante, Kundry, Ptolema—she has many names, as well. The Sino LDTC ferrying her is now less than eight sols out. The Egyptian racing towards her. An unforeseen inconvenience. In no way at all a calamity, no, but still an unfortunate occurrence to force the White Woman's hand. It tries her patience, and patience has been the key for so long that she cannot even recall a time before she learned that lesson.

In less than eight sols, the transfer vessel will dock, and they will speak for the first time in . . .

How long has it been?

She answers the question aloud, "One hundred and thirty-nine years."

"Truly?" asks Babbit. "As long as all that?"

When she arrived on the station two months ago, Babbit was assigned the task of seeing to her every need. As has been her wish, he hardly ever leaves her side. The company of anyone is a balm for her sometimes crippling monophobia. A medicine better than any she has ever been prescribed. It doesn't matter that this tall, thin, tow-headed man is only mostly human. Many times, she's resorted to and relied upon the companionship of splices. Besides, Babbit's fast-borrow capabilities saved her the trouble of telling him all the tales he needs to know to carry on useful conversations. And there will be much less fuss when she orders his death, before her flight back to Earth. Easy come, easy go.

"You've never been to Manhattan," she says.

"Ma'am, it was lost before I was born."

"Of course," she replies, and the White Woman holds

up her right hand, absentmindedly running fingertips along the window, tracing the serpentine furrow on the Chasma Boreale. It seems almost as long as her long life, and almost as aimless. *Possessed of direction,* she thinks, *is not to be possessed of purpose.*

"Anyway," she says to Babbit, "we were in Manhattan. I'd only just returned from Sweden. It was that long ago. Almost all the way back at the start."

"As long as all that," he says again.

"I can't begin to understand what she hopes to accomplish, coming here, chasing after me this way."

"Nor can I, ma'am."

"The vessel may be armed. It would be like her, a preemptive strike, sacrificing the whole station and everyone aboard if she believes doing so would accomplish her ends."

"Zealots are extremely dangerous people," says Babbit.

"It can't be that she hopes to *reason* with me. She cannot entertain the notion that she and I have ever shared in common a concept of Reason."

"True believers, I mean," Babbit says.

"I know what you meant."

"Of course, ma'am."

"Maybe she only wishes to bear witness," the White Woman says. "To be present when my king's knight takes her remaining bishop."

Babbit clears his throat. "I expect the Captain will have anticipated the possibility of an attack," he says, then clears his throat once more.

She laughs. "He has done nothing of the sort. There has been no alert, no preparation to intercept or shield. He is sitting and waiting, like a small and frightened animal cowering in the underbrush."

"I was only supposing," admits Babbit.

The White Woman pulls her hand back from the window, and she seems to stare at it for a few seconds. As if in wonder, maybe. Or as if, perhaps, it's been soiled somehow. Then she turns her head and watches Babbit. He lowers his head; he never meets her gaze.

"I have considered holding off on the launch until she boards," she says to him. "Until she is that near."

"Then you've made your decision? To make the drop, I mean."

"I made that decision before I left Xichang. It was only ever a question of when."

"And now you have decided when?"

No one on the *Nautilus-IV,* no one back on Earth, no one in the scattered, hardscrabble colonies below, none of them know why she is here. Few enough know that she *is* here. She was listed on no passenger manifest. They do not know she's ready to call the Egyptian's gambit and move her king's knight. To cast a stone on the still waters.

Not one of them knows the nature of her cargo. No one but Babbit, and he won't talk.

"Now I have decided when," she tells him, and the White Woman shuts her blue eyes and pictures the vial in its plasma-lock cradle, hidden inside a shipment of hardware and foodstuffs bound for Sharonov. The kinetic gravity bomb will detonate at five hundred feet, and the contents of the vial will be aerosolized. The sky will rain corruption, and the corruption will take root in the dome's cisterns and reservoirs.

לַעֲנָה

Wormwood.

Apsinthion.

. . . *and a great star fell from heaven, blazing like a torch . . .*

"Ma'am," says Babbit, not daring to raise his head. "You are certain you will obtain the desired results? There are evacuation protocols, environmental containment procedures—"

. . . *the waters became wormwood . . .*

Here is the day.

"Babbit, I have never in all my life been certain. Which is the point."

She turns back to the window and can almost feel the wild katabatic winds scouring the glaciers and canyons. The White Woman pulls her robes more tightly about herself. She's glad that Babbit is with her. She wants to ask him if he might take for granted that she has never loved, if no one has ever been dear to her. But she doesn't.

Instead, she says again, "Which is the point."

"Yes, ma'am," he says. "Of course."

ACKNOWLEDGMENTS

I do not write in a vacuum, and I should note the more important influences that played a role in my conception and execution of *Black Helicopters*: T. S. Eliot's *The Waste Land*; the works of Lewis Carroll and Charles Hoy Fort; more books on chess than would be practical to list here, but notably Martin Gardner's examination of the "chess problem" in *Through the Looking Glass, and What Alice Found There*; Mark Twain's *The Adventures of Huckleberry Finn*; David Bowie's *Outside* and *Blackstar*; Anne "Poe" Decatur Danielewski's *Haunted*; Funcom's *The Secret World*; J. J. Abrams, Alex Kurtzman, and Roberto Orci's *Fringe*; Grant Morrison's *The Invisibles*; Current 93's *Black Ships Ate the Sky* and *Soft Black Stars*; James Joyce's *Ulysses*; Eleanor Coerr's *Sadako and the Thousand Paper Cranes*; the music of Radiohead, Moby's *Everything Is Wrong*, and the Veils' *Total Depravity*; various works on chaos theory, astronomy, and quantum physics, including Kip S. Thorne's *Black Holes and Time Warps: Einstein's Outrageous Legacy,* John Briggs and F. David Peat's *Turbulent Mirror: An Illustrated Guide to Chaos Theory and the Science of Wholeness,* and P. J. E. Peebles' *Principles of Physical Cosmology*; Leigh Van Valen and other biologists' writings on the Red Queen hypothesis; and Edward Gorey's *The Other Statue.* Very special thanks to Dr. Denise L. Davis (Brown University) for the French translation in Chapter Nine ("Bury Magnets. Swallow the Rapture. [17 Vrishika, 2152]"); to the amazing "Mr. Rook" for the evening games and the afternoon critiques; to my comrade in virtual arms and conspiracy, Vic Ruiz; to my niece, Sonoye Murphy; and to Kathryn A. Pollnac, my original Miss Sixty-Six. The paleontological exploits, misadventures, and disappointments of the "twins" mentioned in the text are all my own, a sharp jab of autobiography. Thanks to William K. Schafer at Subterranean Press, without whom this novella would never have been written, much less published, and also a posthumous thank-you to Peggy Rae Sapienza (1944–2015), who saw that I made it to Arlington County in October 2014. A special thanks to my editor, Jonathan Strahan, and to Katharine Duckett, Irene Gallo, Theresa DeLucci, and everyone else at Tor.com for giving *Black Helicopters* a new lease on life.

AUTHOR'S NOTE FOR THE DEFINITIVE EDITION

Black Helicopters was written between December 4 and December 15, 2012, as a chapbook to accompany my Subterranean Press collection, *The Ape's Wife and Other Stories* (2013). I'd been carrying the story around inside my head for some time, and I admit that it was quite a bit larger than the 25,000-word chapbook that Subterranean Press required of me. So, a number of scenes were left unwritten. When Tor.com expressed an interest in publishing a new edition of the novella, I took the opportunity to sit down and write those "missing" scenes, and they are included here as chapters Six, Twelve, Thirteen, and Fourteen. Chapter Sixteen is also new, but occurred to me only after I'd written *Agents of Dreamland* in the summer of 2015.

Caitlín R. Kiernan
October 18, 2017
Providence, Rhode Island

ABOUT THE AUTHOR

Photograph by Kyle Cassidy

CAITLÍN R. KIERNAN was born near Dublin, Ireland, in 1964 and was raised in Alabama and Florida. She's worked as a vertebrate paleontologist, museum exhibit technician, biology instructor, reproductive rights activist, and drag queen. Her novels include *Silk, Threshold, Low Red Moon, Murder of Angels, Daughter of Hounds, The Red Tree,* and *The Drowning Girl: A Memoir.* She has also published more than two hundred and sixty short stories, anthologized in several collections, including Subterranean Press' two-volume "best of" retrospective of her short fiction, *Two Worlds and In Between* and *Beneath an Oil-Dark Sea.* In the 1990s, she scripted *The Dreaming* for DC Comics/Vertigo and returned to comics in 2011 with *Alabaster: Wolves, Alabaster: Grimmer Tales,* and *Alabaster: The Good, the Bad, and the Bird,* for Dark Horse Comics. She is a two-time recipient of both the World Fantasy Award and the Bram Stoker Award, a four-time recipient of the International Horror Guild Award, and has also received the James Tiptree, Jr. Award and the Locus Award, along with nominations for the Nebula Award, the Mythopoeic Award, the British Fantasy Award, and the Shirley Jackson Award. She studied paleontology, geology, and comparative zoology at both the University of Alabama in Birmingham and the University of Colorado. In 1988, she described a new genus and species of mosasaur, *Selmasaurus russelli,* from Alabama (with S. W. Shannon) and ten years later discovered the first evidence of velociraptorine theropod dinosaurs ("raptors") from the southeastern United States. In 2017, Brown University's John Hay Library established the Caitlín R. Kiernan Papers, archiving juvenilia, manuscripts, artwork, and other material related to her work. She currently lives in Providence, Rhode Island, with her partner, Kathryn A. Pollnac, and two cats.

TOR·COM

Science fiction. Fantasy. The universe.

And related subjects.

*

More than just a publisher's website, *Tor.com*
is a venue for **original fiction, comics,** and
discussion of the entire field of SF and fantasy,
in all media and from all sources. Visit our site
today—and join the conversation yourself.